I0622222

MARCIA LYNN McCLURE

Published by Distractions Ink
P.O. Box 15971
Rio Rancho, NM 87174

©Copyright 2004, 2010, 2012 by M. L. Meyers
A.K.A. Marcia Lynn McClure
Cover Photography by
©Konradbak and ©Solarseven | Dreamstime.com
Cover Design by
Sheri L. Brady | MightyPhoenixDesignStudio.com

Third Printed Edition: 2012

McClure, Marcia Lynn, 1965—
An Old-Fashioned Romance: a novella/by Marcia Lynn McClure.

ISBN: 978-0-9852807-0-3

Library of Congress Control Number: 2012934283

Printed in the United States of America

To Barbara, Dixie, Karen, and Sheri,
See yourselves in my heart, my dears…
My laughter, my beacons of hope and joy,
My cherished friends.
My eternal love to each of you.

CHAPTER ONE

Breck McCall ran her fingers through her long, chestnut hair, sighing heavily as she waited for the traffic light to turn green. If she kept hitting every light on red, she would never make it to work on time. Still, she smiled as she watched the crossing guard motion for the group of distracted children to cross the street. The crossing guard—an elderly man with sparse silvery hair—waved to the children frantically with one hand, holding tightly to the stop sign in his other. Breck giggled, sympathetic as she watched one little red-haired girl tugging on her purple rolling backpack. It tipped over a moment later, of course, and the frantic crossing guard rushed over to help the child right it. The little girl and her purple rolling backpack were off again soon enough, and Breck smiled and waved at the tired traffic guard as the light turned green. She was on her way to work again.

Working at Wilson Investigation seemed the perfect career path for a young woman like Breck—just a week away from being twenty-one. Her coworkers were friendly enough, the work was far more than merely interesting, and it seemed that all should be well with Breck. But somehow, all wasn't well.

Descended from a long line of horse breeders, Breck's father had chosen the life of a big-city attorney instead of following his older brother into the horse business. Her mother and father were happy enough, but Breck had always struggled with city life. She remembered visiting her uncle's ranch as a child—the way she had always felt free, as if she could breathe better out there in southeastern Colorado. Her father had always maintained she reminded him of his grandfather Michael McCall, who had loved the wide-open space of ranching life. Thus, Breck figured she was that child in every family who should have been born in a different era. But reality was that farming and ranching were vanishing lifestyles. And one didn't easily go from being a big-city girl, employed by one of the top detective agencies in the West, to plopping into the well-worn blue jeans of a farm girl. And so, Breck had finished her degree at Colorado State and had found a job at Wilson.

As she stepped off the elevator on the fourteenth floor, Breck heard the sounds of morning at the office. She could hear the copy machines and printers whirring away and low voices steeped in phone conversation— inhaled the familiar scent of stale doughnuts and old coffee.

"Good morning, Breck," Patty greeted from her seat behind the reception desk. "Having a good one?"

Patty was a sweet, pleasant-natured brunette

woman of about forty-five, the main receptionist at Wilson.

"Yeah. And you?" Breck said.

"Fair enough. Mr. Henshaw has an appointment today."

Mr. Henshaw was a young, recently divorced man, a client of Mr. Wilson's. Patty thought he was the hottest thing since jalapeño bean dip.

Breck giggled and said, "Well, then your day should be a good one!"

Patty's smile widened, and she nodded, seeming to remember something a moment later. "Mr. Thatcher is already in this morning," she said. "He doesn't look like he's had a minute of sleep. Probably staking out a case on his own again."

"Probably," Breck agreed. Mr. Reese Thatcher was not only Breck's boss but also the handsomest man a woman had ever seen—and a bachelor. It was, quite often, difficult to work with him and not stare in awe at his good looks. He was the one reason Breck looked forward to going to work each weekday morning at Wilson Investigation—not that she wasn't well paid, for she was. However, her soul yearned for freedom somehow. But whenever she set eyes on Reese Thatcher, another emotion washed over her—euphoria!

"Have a good one, Patty," Breck called over her shoulder as she passed the reception area and headed for her desk.

"You too," came Patty's cheerful reply.

Setting her purse in the lower drawer of her desk,

Breck tapped her computer keypad to signal her monitor display. The cool breezes of October had left her cheeks rosy and her disposition refreshed. She was ready for another day at the old grind. She noted that Mr. Thatcher had already set a pile of scribbled-on papers atop her desk. No doubt he'd been making notes all night again while he sat in his car staking out someone who was up to some dirty deed.

Breck sighed, feeling sorry for the handsome, brooding man who had to spend so much of his time with dishonest people who could not be trusted.

"Morning, Breck," Reese Thatcher mumbled as he stepped out of his office at that very moment.

"Good morning, Mr. Thatcher," Breck greeted as the scowling man approached her desk. Even scowling he was gorgeous—like some mix between a young Elvis Presley and a young John Stamos.

He ran his fingers through his black hair and forced a considerate smile as he said, "I tossed some notes on your desk when I came in this morning. Can you get them entered for me as soon as possible? I've already forgotten what's on them."

"I sure can," she answered.

He handed her a large black envelope next. "These pictures go in the Allen file. Michael Allen should be calling sometime this morning. Just let him know they're here whenever he wants his attorney to pick them up, okay?" he mumbled, running his fingers through his thick, ebony hair again.

"Sure," Breck answered. She felt a hard lump form

in her throat, her stomach churning a bit. She'd done enough work on Mrs. Allen's case to know what must be in the black envelope—photos of Mr. Allen consorting with another woman. These kinds of cases always made Breck sick to her stomach, and unfortunately, there were far too many of them.

"Detective Taylor should be dropping some stuff by later too," Mr. Thatcher continued. "Bring it right in, would ya?"

"I will," Breck agreed.

She felt a slight blush rise to her cheeks as Reese Thatcher smiled at her a moment and said, "You look nice today, Breck."

"Thank you, Mr. Thatcher." Breck took his compliments not too much to heart, however. He always told old Mr. Wilson's assistant that she looked nice too. Mr. Wilson's secretary had been with him for forty years and was almost seventy—a fairly grouchy lady with a straight line for a smile and a perpetual frown.

"Another pumpkin sweater, I see," he noted.

"Yep," Breck admitted. Still, she was flattered that he would notice her passion for sweaters with pumpkins or orange patterns woven into them. "It is October, after all, Mr. Thatcher."

The smile he directed at her broadened. "Is it?" he teased. "And me without a pumpkin sweater to my name."

Reese Thatcher couldn't ignore the warm feeling

sweeping over him at the sight of his attractive assistant dressed in yet another sweater paying homage to the ultimate orange squash. Over the past couple of weeks, he'd begun to wonder how much of her paychecks she spent on pumpkin-themed sweaters and where in the world she was able to find so many. It was one of the most adorable things about her lately, he noted to himself. But he buried that thought, not only quickly but deep.

Breck's smile broadened too at his teasing. He turned, and she couldn't help noticing how nicely his jeans fit, how the fitted, ribbed knit shirt he wore complemented his muscular build and broad shoulders.

With that black hair and those blue eyes, you'd look ridiculous in a pumpkin sweater, she thought. But she'd be willing to bet he'd look great in a red Christmassy one.

When he finally walked into his office, closing the door behind him, Breck exhaled a sigh of relief. Oh, how he rattled her! The epitome of the tall, dark, and handsome cliché, Reese Thatcher was one of those guys that a girl sees only one or two of in her entire life! He was tall, broad-shouldered, and in excellent shape physically. His eyes were a kind of light, light blue—almost sky blue—and his hair the deepest black Breck had ever seen in real life. His perfectly straight, perfectly white teeth added a movie-star quality to his smile, and he was simply the most handsome man Breck had ever seen! Not to mention that he was kind, well-mannered, and as masculine as they came.

Breck, in contrast, felt very plain. Green eyes, brown hair, medium height—not much to brag about. She did have a good figure, but still, she saw nothing unusually striking about herself. Thus, a man like Reese Thatcher intimidated the life out of her! She knew that every girl in the office daydreamed about him, and—the truth be told—she was no different.

Imagine kissing him, she thought to herself. *I'd drop dead on the spot, for sure.*

Sighing and trying to dispel any daydreams of being Reese Thatcher's girlfriend, Breck filed Mr. Allen's envelope in her desk file drawer and proceeded to put her phone headset on just as the phone rang.

With a, "Good morning. Wilson Investigation, Reese Thatcher's office. May I help you?" Breck's day at work officially began.

The morning was uneventful at best. Breck worked most of the day preparing the information Reese had gathered for Mrs. Allen's file, and it put her in a rather foul mood. She kept thinking that someone ought to string Mr. Allen up by his toenails and torture him for cheating on his sweet wife. And the fact the couple had a brand-new baby only served to further infuriate her. By the time her lunch hour rolled around, Breck was more than ready for a break. And it promised to be a fun one—for she was meeting her four best friends downtown at Marcelli's.

Marcelli's was Breck's very favorite restaurant! It boasted the best Italian food in three states and with affordable prices. Plus, Sherryl, Trixie, Kay, and Barb were meeting her there. In fact, she'd scheduled herself an hour and a half for lunch—to allow more time to visit with her friends.

Lunch with these girls was always an adventure! Nothing ever went smoothly, mostly because they were all laughing so hard they couldn't eat. The tips they all left were more than generous—because each of them felt a bit guilty for being overly flirty with the waiter of the day. Yep! Breck looked forward to time with her four dearest friends more than anything. She knew the girls would help lift her out of her *I wish someone would flog Mr. Allen* mood into a *I'll just enjoy looking at my handsome boss* frame of mind once again.

Before the waiter had even shown Breck the table where her friends waited, she could hear them. Barb's laugh was literally contagious, and Breck heard herself giggle as she heard its magical melody drifting from one corner of the room.

No doubt Trixie (her real name being Marie) was already busy sculpting puppies with some bread and olive oil. Trixie couldn't leave her food alone to save her life! She was forever sculpting puppies, penguins, and even North America out of bread, leftover desserts, and pancakes. She was good at it too! Breck had often wondered why Trixie didn't take to sculpting with some substance more lasting and durable than leftover restaurant food.

Kay would have a list of books as long as her arm ready to share. Kay loved to read, and her sole purpose in life had become trying to find a book for Breck that would outdo Breck's beloved and favorite book, *The Highwayman of Tanglewood*. Kay knew it was a daunting task—one most likely never to be achieved. Still, Kay had given Breck some fantastic reading material over the years—even though nothing would ever beat out *The Highwayman of Tanglewood* in Breck's heart.

And then there was Sherryl. Sherryl was the "up-to-no-gooder" of the group. A well-known photographer by trade, Sherryl would inevitably have the girls up to their necks in mischief by the end of lunch. Whether it was flirting shamelessly with some poor waiter, trying to solve the love-life concerns of some unsuspecting waitress, or simply cracking jokes all through lunch until everyone had indigestion, Sherryl was the clown of the clan.

Yes, as Breck approached the table and saw her friends, smiling faces ablaze with mirth, she knew this would, once again, be a lunch to remember.

"Did you pinch your boss's butt yet, Breck?" Sherryl inquired as Breck took her seat at the table. As usual, the waiters had the foresight to sit this group of women out of the way of normal, everyday folks.

"I could get sued for that, Sherr," Breck reminded with a giggle.

"So what?" Trixie said. "Your dad's a lawyer."

Everyone laughed, and Kay hugged Breck as she sat down. As always, Breck sighed as she scanned the faces of her beloved chums. These girls were real. There was nothing false or arrogant about them, and Breck loved them with all her heart—depended on them to help her through the ugly parts of life.

"I don't know how you keep your hands off that man," Barb said, shaking her head.

"I admit it…it's hard," Breck sighed. "Especially since it's painfully obvious that he wants me," she sighed dramatically.

Everyone laughed, and lunch began with Trixie's proud display of her latest restaurant appetizer sculpture—Italian bread smooshed and flattened into the shape of Texas.

The hour passed too quickly, and Breck's sides were aching from laughing so hard. Barb had laughed so hard at one point that the gulp of water she'd just taken left her body by way of her nose. And so it was that, with an overly full stomach and a heart full of mirth, Breck glanced over to where their waiter was seating a new set of patrons.

Her very audible gasp caused her friends to follow her gaze.

"Oh my heck!" Kay exclaimed in a whisper. "It's him!"

"Oh my heck, it is!" Trixie confirmed.

Indeed, sitting at a table just across the room was none other than Reese Thatcher! Breck felt hot beads of perspiration accumulate on her forehead as she looked and noted the rather beautiful blonde that was with him.

"And he's with a woman!" Sherryl exclaimed in a hushed tone.

"That ain't no woman," Barb corrected. "If she's with Breck's man…she's a hoochie."

"Ssshh! You guys! He'll hear us," Breck warned.

"Oh my heck! He *is* gorgeous," Kay whispered, ignoring Breck's warning. "Breck…you have to marry him!"

"For Pete's sake, Kay," Breck scolded, slouching down in her seat. "He'll hear you!"

"You definitely have to pinch his butt," Trixie added, winking at Breck. Breck couldn't fault them at all for teasing her. For were the shoe on the other foot—and it had been in the past—she would have been just as bad.

"Oh my heck! Oh my heck!" Sherryl warned. "He's looking over here!"

"I wonder why," Breck growled, unable to help but smile at her silly friends.

"Well, sit up straight, Breck," Barb ordered. "You don't want him to think you're a sloucher, for crying out loud."

Breck thought she might nearly drop dead when she heard Kay say, "Oh my heck! Oh my heck! He's coming over, Breck! Oh my heck!"

Breck plastered on a fake smile and looked up just in time to see none other than Reese Thatcher standing over her.

"Well, hello, Breck," he greeted.

"Hello, Mr. Thatcher," she managed to sputter.

"Girls' day out, huh?" he asked, waiting for an introduction.

"Yep," Breck confirmed. Still, she was completely tongue-tied and couldn't respond any further.

Fortunately, or rather unfortunately, Sherryl's tongue was all too loose.

"Well, hello, Mr. Thatcher," Sherryl greeted. "We're Breck's idiot friends."

"Nice to meet you all," Reese Thatcher said, smiling, obviously amused. "So...uh...is this an official meeting of the Pumpkin Sweater Club?"

Breck closed her eyes for a moment, horrified as she, only then, realized she and every one of her friends wore sweaters with some sort of pumpkin design on them. Reese Thatcher smiled and looked to Breck.

"Um...no, sir. We just all like...pumpkin sweaters," she explained.

"Is that your girlfriend, Mr. Thatcher?" Barb asked. Barb was known as the blunt one of the group. She didn't believe in wasting time. *Cut to the chase and just find out what you want to know* was her motto. Breck was mortified—wanted to scream with embarrassment. However, Reese grinned, amused by the woman's brazenness.

"No...just a friend," he answered.

Breck was silently scolding herself for being so relieved that the woman wasn't his girlfriend. Further she was irritated with herself for caring so much.

Reese smiled at her, and Breck was certain that he pitied her for her discomfort. He said, "Well, I'll leave you ladies to your dessert. It was nice to meet you all." Then, winking at Breck, he added, "See you back at the office, Miss Pumpkin Sweater Club President."

"Okay," Breck managed.

Everyone at the table was silent—all five sets of eyes intent on Reese Thatcher as he sauntered away. And then Breck knew it would start. And it did.

"I cannot believe you haven't pinched that rear end," Trixie teased.

"I cannot believe you haven't thrown him down on your desk and smooched him!" Kay added.

"I cannot believe that he noticed we were all wearing pumpkin sweaters," was Sherryl's contribution.

"I cannot believe that you didn't run over there and claw that hoochie's eyes out...just a friend or not!" Barb concluded.

I cannot believe was a sort of verbal game that Breck and her friends played quite often during their conversations and adventures. And it was Breck's turn.

"I cannot believe that you guys are so crazy!" Breck exclaimed in a whisper. Then they all started to giggle, and Breck relaxed once more.

Reese couldn't help but glance over to the table where Breck and her friends were finishing up their lunch. He'd never heard such giggling and goings-on, and it made him smile. He suspected that Breck was completely caught off guard by his presence at Marcelli's, and he had enjoyed the look on her face when one of her friends had askÓed if the woman with him were his girlfriend.

Of course, he knew that the woman with him, Meagan Jetta, wanted to be his girlfriend. She'd made it quite obvious many, many times. But Meagan wasn't for him. She was nice, pretty, and fun—enjoyable to go to lunch with—as a friend. But he wanted nothing more serious where she was concerned.

In fact, he felt bad that he kept glancing to Breck's table, his mind wandering from the conversation he was having with Meagan.

"Your secretary is a little obnoxious, Reese," Meagan said. "And what's with all the pumpkin sweaters anyway?"

Reese smiled. He wasn't angry with Meagan. He had neglected their conversation since seeing Breck at the restaurant.

Picking up his glass, he took a drink of water and said, "Apparently it's a Pumpkin Sweater Club meeting."

Meagan rolled her eyes and breathed, "Whatever." Then looking at her watch, she gasped and said, "Oh! I've got to run, Reese! I've got an appointment at Jenkins and Jenkins in ten minutes. Thanks for lunch."

"Sure," Reese said as Meagan hopped up and left the table.

He felt guilty for being so relieved that she was gone. Now he could spy on Breck and her friends in private. However, when he looked over to their table, it was to see Breck waving and walking away. He watched as her friends lingered, whispering among themselves and glancing over at him. One of them hopped up and went to the window that overlooked the parking lot. And then, much to his dismay and delight, the four women rose from their table and began walking toward him.

When they reached his table, it was the skinny blonde who found the nerve to speak first.

"Um...excuse us. Mr. Thatcher?" the skinny blonde said.

"Yeah," Reese said, his curiosity more than piqued.

"Hi, I'm Sherryl Foster," the skinny blonde began, "Breck McCall's friend."

"Yes, we've met. Did you forget already?" Reese teased.

"Oh, no. Of course not," the woman assured him.

"What can I do for you ladies?"

The four young women giggled like high school cheerleaders talking to the captain of the football team—their eyes lit up with mischievous excitement.

"Well," Sherryl Foster began, "Breck's birthday is next Friday."

"Her twenty-first birthday," the dark brunette added. "I'm Trixie," she whispered aside to him.

"Yes," Sherryl confirmed, then continued, "and we've just come up with the greatest idea for her birthday dinner. And...and..."

"And we were hoping you'd be willing to help us out," the lighter brunette finished.

"Oh, really?" Reese asked.

"Barb," the lighter brunette told him. This was getting interesting. He was very intrigued. A surprise for Breck's birthday with these four chatterboxes involved would certainly be something to behold.

"Kay," the other blonde said. She nodded and then continued, "Now, don't worry. It doesn't involve a giant cake or you in nothing but a bow tie and your underwear."

Reese chuckled. "Well, that's good to know."

"Although," the darker brunette said to the lighter one, "that *would* be a nice finale for Breck's birthday dinner."

Reese chuckled as he watched their faces. It seemed they actually considered the idea for a moment—then realized exactly what had been suggested and began shaking their heads in unison.

"Yeah, yeah, yeah," the skinny blonde said. "A bit over the edge for a public display."

"For Breck anyway," the lighter brunette noted.

These friends of Breck's were funny, and it made him wish he could've been a fly on the wall when Breck had been with them at lunch.

"What *is* your plan, ladies?" Reese asked. He grinned, amused at the way they all looked one to the other in such a mischievous, conspiratorial manner.

"Well, Mr. Reese Thatcher," the dark brunette began, "Kay here is a fabulous seamstress."

Thirty minutes later, Reese Thatcher sat in his pickup

in Marcelli's parking lot. He couldn't believe he'd agreed to be involved in such a mess! For a moment he felt sorry for Breck. The attention would, no doubt, mortify her. Still, a girl who wore pumpkin-themed sweaters every day in October and owned friends who would concoct such a scheme—there was definitely more to Breck McCall than met the eye. Of course, he'd suspected that from the moment he'd hired her.

Still, he wondered what on earth had gotten into him. Shaking his head, he turned the key in the ignition. It was about time he did something fun—something to take his mind off the ghosts in his past, the muck he was knee-deep in at work. Pumpkin sweaters—that gave him another idea. Picking up his cell, he dialed and waited for an answer at the other end.

"Hi, Mom," he greeted. "I need a favor."

Her lunch with the girls had completely revitalized Breck. Back at work and sitting at her desk once more, she felt refreshed and not so resentful about the condition of the world. She wished she could meet the girls more often, but at least she had dinner next Friday with them to look forward to. She smiled, knowing they'd make her twenty-first birthday dinner at Marcelli's a memorable one indeed. She suspected they had something wild up their sleeves, and it would be hard to wait over a week to find out what it was.

"Seems like you've got a good group of friends there, Breck," Reese Thatcher said as he approached her desk.

Breck felt herself blush. It had been so startling to see him at Marcelli's—so irritating to see him with that woman—so frightening to sit and wonder what her friends might say when they met him. Her emotions were in turmoil. Not to mention he looked particularly handsome at that moment. Lunch at Marcelli's seemed to agree with just about anybody.

"Yeah. They're a bunch of fun," she said.

"They certainly seem to be," he said, smiling. Breck blushed, flustered—wondering what else he'd witnessed of her luncheon at Marcelli's.

He turned to walk into his office but paused and looked back at her.

Pointing an index finger at her, he said, "Did I tell you, 'Nice pumpkin sweater,' yet today?"

Breck smiled at his teasing manner. "Yes, sir. You did."

He winked at her and closed his office door behind him.

He seemed oddly relaxed, Breck mused. But the smile left her face when she began to wonder if it were simply lunch at Marcelli's that had given him a lift. Or was it the woman—rather, the hoochie—he'd been lunching with?

CHAPTER TWO

Breck's twenty-first birthday dawned on a perfectly crisp and cool autumn morning. October's end brought with it a feel of frost in the air. Tired trees were shedding the last of their leaves of reds and gold, and piles of pumpkins dotted the front porches of Colorado suburbia. Breck felt more lighthearted than usual as she waited for the elevator doors to open onto the fourteenth floor and the Wilson Investigation offices.

In fact, she felt so excited—anxiously anticipating dinner at Marcelli's with Trixie, Sherryl, Barb, and Kay—that when the elevator doors did open at last, she rushed forward, plowing into Marty Sprague from accounting. The files Marty had been holding under his arms went flying everywhere, scattering quite efficiently over the floor in front of the elevator.

"Oh, Marty!" Breck exclaimed. "I'm so sorry. I wasn't paying attention."

Marty smiled down at Breck. "That's okay, Breck. No problem."

Breck returned Marty's friendly smile, on her guard however—for it was unspoken but public knowledge throughout the office that Marty more than admired Breck. He was a handsome one too—tall, very well built, and with brown hair and green eyes that flashed like emeralds when he was looking at something he liked. And his eyes were certainly flashing as he watched Breck drop to her knees and begin gathering his papers.

He hunkered down to help her retrieve the innards of his files, and Breck felt the heat of his stare on the top of her head.

"Rumor has it that today's your birthday," he said as they scooped up papers.

"Well, for once the ol' rumor mill is correct," Breck admitted. Even though Marty's attention unnerved her a bit, he'd never made any inappropriate advances toward her. He'd asked her out several times, and Breck had enjoyed his company well enough, but that was all—casual friendship. No butterflies took flight in her stomach when he entered the room; no goose bumps broke over her flesh at his touch. And that was what Breck wanted—butterflies and goose bumps.

"Not to spoil the surprise," Marty began, "but they've got a cake and are all waiting in the break room for you. The standard birthday snacks here at Wilson."

Breck smiled, pleased to work for a firm that recognized employees in such a kind manner.

"How neat," she said, smiling.

"I thought you'd think so," Marty chuckled.

All the papers having been gathered, Marty pushed the elevator down button on the wall and waited for his transportation to arrive.

"So…happy birthday, Breck," he told her, smiling.

"Thank you," she said, returning his smile.

The elevator doors opened, and Marty stepped in, turning to face her again. "Oh," he added, "and that's a nice pumpkin sweater you're wearing today."

Breck giggled and tossed him a friendly wave as the elevator doors closed. Sighing heavily, she turned to greet Patty. Patty wore her familiar, captivating smile that seemed to please and comfort anyone who saw it. A person couldn't help but smile back at Patty—her smile was that agreeable.

"He's sweet on you, you know," Patty told her.

"Sweet on me, Patty?" Breck giggled. "Patty, you sound like my grandma."

"Well, he is," Patty assured her.

Breck's smile faded a bit at the thought of what a handsome and kind young man Marty was. Why couldn't she like him? He was perfect. Wasn't he? No—sadly he wasn't. Not when you stood him next to Reese Thatcher. And that, after all, was the whole problem. It seemed no matter how nice a man was— how handsome or polite—Breck kept comparing him to her boss—her gorgeous, kind, out-of-reach boss. Reese Thatcher possessed a sort of vintage masculinity. It would be hard for any man to compete with that rare quality. Still, Breck knew how unobtainable Reese was to her, so it bothered her that his presence in her life would keep her from gravitating to a good man like Marty. But fact was fact—and Marty just wasn't the zinger.

"And a happy birthday to you, Breck!" Patty added.

"Thanks, Patty," Breck said. It was nice to have such kind and sincere birthday wishes—two already and she'd only just stepped off the elevator.

"I've got a little something for you," Patty told her, rising from her seat behind the reception desk and handing Breck a small package.

"Patty!" Breck exclaimed. "You didn't need to do that."

Patty smiled and nodded. "I know. But I wanted to. You're just such a sweet girl, Breck. You deserve to have some special attention on your birthday."

Breck giggled. "Can I open it now?"

Patty smiled. "Of course."

Breck admired the pretty wrapping of the package for a moment—pink paper with lavender and yellow ribbon tied around it. Then she quickly slid the ribbon off and tore away the paper to reveal a white box. Opening the box, she withdrew its contents and gasped with surprise and delight.

"Oh, Patty!" she exclaimed as she held the lovely snow globe in her hand. The globe housed a dainty fairy with wings of gold and green, sitting on a large pumpkin. Furthermore, instead of the traditional white snow that usually furled around when one shook or turned such a globe upside down, swirling Patty's gifted globe revealed tiny red, orange, and yellow leaves raining down on the pretty autumn fairy and her pumpkin throne. It was so beautiful and such an obviously personal gift that it brought tears to Breck's eyes for a moment.

"Patty," Breck said in a whisper, "it's the most beautiful thing I've ever seen. Truly!"

Patty smiled, delighted with Breck's reaction.

"Well," she began, "when Mr. Thatcher pointed out to me the other day that you'd been wearing pumpkin sweaters all month…well, I saw this in that little gift shop on Burlington, and…well…you just had to have it!"

Breck felt her heart rather leap in her bosom at the knowledge that not only had Reese Thatcher noticed her pumpkin sweaters, he'd talked about them to Patty. Impulsively she threw her arms around Patty's neck, hugging her.

"Thank you so much, Patty," Breck told her. "You'll never know how much I love this and how much your thoughtfulness means."

Patty returned her embrace and then said, "You deserve it, Breck. You're the nicest girl here." Breck smiled as Patty smiled at her. "There's something different about you, you know," Patty told her. "You're…well, it's as if you…I don't know. It's like you're from somewhere else…somewhere other than a big city. I think your heart is sweeter…more kind than most."

Breck smiled—touched beyond description at the woman's tender words.

"Now, you get on into your office. Mr. Thatcher was pacing the floors early this morning. I'm sure something is up with that Allen case. I heard him talking to Mrs. Allen on his cell as he stepped off the elevator," Patty told her.

Breck smiled. "Thank you again, Patty. It's so beautiful."

"You're very welcome, Breck," Patty said.

When Breck arrived at her desk, Reese was nowhere to be seen. So she set her lovely new snow globe—or rather, leaf globe—on her desk and tried to get to work. But she found it hard to concentrate. All she could think about was dinner at Marcelli's that night with the girls and, of course, Reese Thatcher. Seeing him at Marcelli's with an unknown woman the week before had greatly disturbed Breck. For some reason, the jealousy she felt every time she thought of it churned in her like an intestinal virus. She hadn't been able to get past it all week, and it bothered her. Furthermore, the physical reactions her body had been having in Reese's presence had also increased over the past few days. She felt rather shaken whenever he was around—nervous, giggly, uncertain of herself. It was driving her nuts!

And where was he anyway? Patty had made it sound as if he'd be waiting right there for her, ready to rant and rave about the Allen case.

Breck's phone rang then, and she answered it to find Barb on the other end.

"Happy birthday, Breck!" her friend greeted. "Mr. Wonderful around there close?"

"Haven't seen him yet," Breck answered, lowering her voice.

"Don't forget...we're picking you up at six-thirty sharp tonight," Barb needlessly reminded her.

"How could I forget," Breck giggled. "I can't wait!"

At that very moment, Reese rounded the corner. A severe frown wrinkled his brow, and he was heading straight for Breck's desk, his eyes deadlocked on her.

"Gotta go, Barb," Breck whispered.

"Okay," Barb said. "But it's your birthday today, Breck, and he owes you something. Be sure to pinch his—"

Breck hung up the phone before Barb had finished, for Reese now stood directly before her, glaring down at her—fury all too evident in his expression.

"Breck, will you get Michael Allen on the phone for me?" he growled. "I have something to say to him and can't find his number."

Breck sighed and adjusted the headset mike at her mouth. Reese was mad! She'd seen him like this several times before—usually when husbands or wives had done each other wrong. And fortunately she knew how to handle him—thus keeping him out of trouble.

"I will, Mr. Thatcher," she said calmly, "if you really want me to."

"I really want you to," Reese grumbled. Still, she could see him calming down a bit.

"Okay. But remember...you don't want to do anything that might jeopardize Mrs. Allen or her case in any way," she reminded him.

Reese drew in and exhaled a deep breath, closed his

eyes for a moment, and then tilted his head to one side as he looked at Breck and grinned.

"Trying to keep me out of jail again?" he asked.

"Yes, sir. Trying," Breck answered, smiling at him.

She startled when Reese placed his fists on her desk and leaned toward her for a moment. Then, shaking his head and straightening to his full height once again, he said, "That man's an...idiot."

Breck couldn't stop the grin that spread across her face. She'd heard Reese call Michael Allen a lot of things while he was talking to various people in his office. *Idiot* was the tamest term he'd used.

"Yes, sir. He is," she agreed.

Another deep sigh to further calm his temper and he turned toward his office.

"Oh, wait," he said, however. Pointing an index finger at Breck, he said. "Wait right there."

Breck smiled. He was her boss—where did he think she was going? He disappeared into his office, only to return a moment later with a badly wrapped gift in his hands.

Breck felt her cheeks go crimson with a hot blush as he held the gift out to her and said, "Happy birthday."

"Thank you," she breathed as she accepted the gift from him.

"I wrapped it myself," he boasted, and Breck giggled. She loved a man who wrapped a gift so that it looked worse than a kindergartener's first attempt. First of all, it was purely masculine to be all thumbs with wrapping paper, tape, and scissors. Second, she'd always felt that a man attempting to wrap a gift on his own showed sincere care. Oh, it was fine in her book for a man to have his wife, his daughters, or a department store wrapping service fancy up his gifts. But attempting to wrap a present on his own—there was an adorable man!

"It's beautiful!" Breck lied as she noted the pink bow so obviously over-taped on the orange wrapping paper.

"I think it looks pretty good too," he said with the sweetest boyish pride. "But open it up. I want to see if it fits."

Breck giggled. Another cute man thing—unconsciously revealing the contents of a gift. For appearance's sake—after all, he had expended quite a lot of effort on his wrapping—Breck opened the gift carefully. She was unable to stifle another nervous giggle when she was fairly certain that whatever Reese had sheltered inside hadn't really come from "Uncle Ben's Fish and Tackle," as the stickers on the box indicated.

"You are gonna love this," Reese said, chuckling. Breck looked up at him, amazed by the mischievous twinkle in his eyes. He nodded and winked at her, biting his lower lip in anticipation. For Pete's sake—she was sure he was more excited than she was!

Breck's heart began to hammer rather intensely as she opened the box. Immediately upon seeing the color of its contents, she gasped, guessing at once what the item was.

"Oh, Mr. Thatcher!" She was so delighted, she

nearly squealed the exclamation. An orange mound of knitted yarn was badly folded and cached in the fish-and-tackle store box.

With a chuckle, Reese told her, "It's a pumpkin sweater!" He chuckled, obviously very proud of his clever gift. "And I know for a fact that you don't have this one."

Breck's hands began to tremble as she took the sweater from the box and unfolded it across the top of her desk. It was truly beautiful! Knitted out of the softest orange yarn, it had several small pumpkins woven into the pattern here and there—each embellished with three leaves at its stem and accented by twisty green vine remnants. It was truly the most beautifully crafted—most beautiful in every way—pumpkin sweater that Breck had ever seen.

"Oh, Mr. Thatcher," she breathed in awe. "It's so perfect!"

She felt goose bumps break over her body as he knelt down beside her at her desk—his arm brushing her shoulder for a moment. She could smell him instantly too—the soft, masculine scent of Speed Stick and aftershave filling her senses.

"It's nice, isn't it?" he asked. Then looking to her, their faces only inches apart, he added, "Don't you want to know how I found a pumpkin sweater you didn't already have?" Breck held her breath. He was so close—so gorgeous! She could feel the warmth of his arm as he rested it on the back of her chair. Five inches forward and she could've kissed him smack on the mouth!

"Um…yes," she stammered.

"Well," he began, his eyes holding her mesmerized gaze, "at first I wondered if maybe you were sick of pumpkin sweaters. You know what I mean?" Breck nodded, intrigued and delighted by his boasting over his finding the perfect gift for her. "Like…you know…a guy…he finds a sports logo he likes, and he can stick with it for, like, forty years, you know?" Breck nodded again, amused by his analogy. "But a girl…no offense, Breck…but girls can be pretty fickle." Breck could only nod again. "However, when I saw you and your friends at the restaurant the other day…every one of you wearing some sort of pumpkin fanatic sweater."

Breck giggled at the memory.

"I figured…you're a collector. And collectors never have enough of whatever they collect. Right?"

"Right," Breck breathed again.

"So," Reese continued, "I called my mom."

Breck's heart began to slip into the pit of her stomach. He'd sent his mom shopping for her birthday present? All she could visualize then was the woman wearing herself ragged by running around trying to find an obligatory birthday gift for her son's secretary.

"Oh," Breck managed, forcing a smile. "It was so kind of her to look—" she began.

"No, no, no," Reese interrupted. "She knitted it just for you. It's a one of a kind."

"What?" Breck asked, her emotions bouncing back and forth so quickly it was giving her a headache.

"Yeah. My mom's a great knitter," he told her. "Look," he said taking the collar of the sweater and turning it down. "See there." He pointed to a small hand-sewn tag on the inside back of the sweater. "Made with love by Marjie Thatcher," he read.

Breck felt tears welling in her eyes. What a special thing he'd done! Sure, it had imposed on his mother, but not the way Breck had at first imagined. This was different! Asking his mother to make such a unique and individual gift? It was unbelievable.

Reese looked at Breck, studying her face for a moment. As Breck willed her tears to stay in her eyes and not escape down her cheeks, Reese said, "You like it, huh?"

"I love it," Breck admitted, her voice cracking a bit and betraying the depth of the emotion she felt.

Reese allowed a triumphant smile to spread across his face, a deep sigh of satisfaction escaping his lungs as he stood.

"I can't...I can't ever thank you enough," Breck told him. "Or your mother! What incredible sacrifice she must've made."

Reese chuckled. "Naw. She loves it," he assured her. "I can just see her now...sitting in her lounge chair, orange yarn and knitting needles flying at the speed of light." Breck smiled at the vision Reese's mind must be conjuring for him.

"Thank you, Mr. Thatcher," Breck said.

Reese smiled and winked at her. "You're welcome, Breck." Then—and Breck thought she might drop dead on the spot from the rapture of the sensation his touch sent through her—Reese Thatcher brushed her left cheek with the back of his hand and added, "Happy birthday."

"Thank you," was all she could manage. With a final grin in her direction, Reese Thatcher disappeared into his office.

The moment his office door was closed, Breck blinked, causing a flood of withheld tears to stream down her cheeks. Quickly, she wiped at them with the backs of her hands. Neatly folding the sweater, she placed it back inside the Uncle Ben's Fish and Tackle box before she rushed to the ladies room to splash some cool water on her face.

After five or ten minutes of regaining her composure in the bathroom, Breck was back at her desk, trying to get some work done. But the feel of Reese Thatcher so close to her as he'd been when he'd hunkered down by her chair—the knowledge that he'd been so thoughtful about a gift for her birthday—all of it kept her stomach in knots for the rest of the morning.

Breck had begun to fall in love with her boss the first moment she met him six months before when she interviewed for the position as his assistant. But during the past few weeks her feelings for him had erupted into a state that was beginning to worry her. And as she sat at her desk a few minutes before lunch—reading the handwritten sweater-washing instructions that Reese's mother had placed in one sleeve of the sweater—she began to feel frightened. He'd break her heart and not even know it.

Her anxious thoughts were interrupted when Patty came rather bouncing up to her desk and said, "Ready for lunch, Breck? The support staff is all downstairs waiting already."

It was a common practice at Wilson Investigation for all support staff members to take one another out to lunch on any given member's birthday. Breck had been excited that morning at the prospect of lunch with her friends at work. But since Reese had gifted her the sweater earlier in the day, her emotions were such a jumble that she wondered if she'd be able to settle down and enjoy lunch at all.

Fortunately, she did. The little Mexican restaurant Patty had reserved for Breck's lunch provided quite the perfect party atmosphere. Many of her friends even brought gifts. And, of course, she was forced to wear the sequin-sloshed sombrero as the restaurant employees sang "Feliz Cumpleaños" to her.

Still, returning to the office left Breck feeling quite unsettled. She wondered if perhaps it was simply her excitement about her impending dinner with friends that night. But that theory was quickly squelched when Reese returned from lunch.

"Did you have a nice birthday lunch?" he asked

her as he walked—rather sauntered—toward his own office.

"Yes, thank you," Breck answered a bit too politely.

"Did they make you wear the hat?" he chuckled.

"Of course," she admitted.

"Did they take a Polaroid picture of you in it and stick it up on the restaurant wall of humiliation?"

Breck nodded.

"Good," he chuckled. "Every one of us has been humiliated that way. It's about time you joined the ranks."

"I want a word with you, Reese Thatcher!" an angry voice shouted.

Reese frowned and turned toward the angry man storming his way toward them from the hallway linking the office spaces with the reception desk. Breck drew in her breath, unhappy at seeing Michael Allen suddenly standing in front of her desk, glaring at Reese.

"Go home, Allen," Reese growled. "Oh, wait," he added, his voice thick with sarcasm, "you don't have a home, do you? You kicked it right out the window."

Breck pushed her chair back from her desk and stood up, pressing the security button on her phone.

"Security," came Dave Pullman's voice on the other end.

"Dave," Breck whispered, "would you come down to Mr. Thatcher's office immediately?" There was no pause, simply a dial tone indicating that Dave was on his way.

"And what are you doing with my wife, Thatcher?" Mr. Allen shouted. "Providing the rebound vessel?"

"I am gonna kick your sorry—" Reese growled a moment before Breck climbed over the top of her desk and planted herself squarely between the two men. She put her hand over Reese's mouth to keep him from delivering a verbal assault that could get him in trouble.

"Go ahead!" Mr. Allen challenged. "I'll sue yours for assault!"

"Mr. Allen," Breck said to the man, turning to face him, "you need to leave. You shouldn't even be here." She could feel Reese's body against her back and knew that she was the only thing keeping him from going at Michael Allen with both fists flying.

"I can be wherever the hell I want to be!" the man shouted at her. Then, taking her chin in his hand, he growled, "You got something going on with him too?" Breck slapped the man's hand away but not in time to keep Reese in line.

"Oh, that's it, man! You're dead!" Reese threatened, taking Breck by the shoulders and moving her aside.

"Come on, coward," Mr. Allen said, trying to provoke Reese further. "You gonna hide behind your secretary all day?"

Breck caught Reese's arm mid-air, only just stopping the brutal punch he'd thrown at Michael Allen.

"Reese!" she shouted. "Reese! Don't let him provoke you. It's what he wants."

Reese pulled his arm from Breck's grasp and looked at her. His eyes were red with fury, his broad chest rising and falling with the heavy breathing of anger. Forcibly, Breck pushed at Reese's chest with all her strength, trying to get him to take a step back. When he finally did, she knew it was not because of the strength of her pushes but rather because he was obeying her.

"You're nothing but a low-life nobody, Thatcher," Allen growled. "Spying on people, taking pictures, and messing with other men's wives."

This time Breck had to turn to face Reese to keep him from going off at the man. Pushing him back against the wall, she took his face in her hands and made him look at her.

"Ignore him, Reese. It's what he wants," she told him as his jaw tightened with anger. "Give Dave a minute, and the guy will be out of here."

As if in answer to her prayers, Dave walked up behind Michael Allen at that very moment.

"Come with me, sir," Dave demanded. Dave Pullman was a huge man! At six foot seven, his size alone would intimidate just about anyone. Add to that the Marine tattoos on his forearms, his flattop haircut, and bulging biceps, and Wilson had just about the most intimidating security guard in the state.

"Yeah, I'm going," Michael Allen growled. But as Dave backed him out of the room, he pointed at Reese and added, "You stay away from my wife. We'll get things worked out without anybody's help."

Reese lurched forward, but Breck put a hand to his chest to stall him. Dave escorted the man from the room, and Breck relaxed the pressure she'd used to hold Reese against the wall.

"You all right, Reese? Breck?" Mr. Wilson asked as he hurried into the room.

"Yeah, yeah. We're fine, Roger," Reese grumbled.

"That right, Breck?" Mr. Wilson asked, obviously not convinced by Reese's appearance.

"Yes, sir," Breck assured him.

"Then you take the rest of the day off, Reese," the older man said. "You need to simmer it down a bit, you hear me?" Reese nodded and sighed. "Okay then. Everybody back to work." Old Mr. Wilson hobbled off, having made his demands.

Breck was startled as she felt Reese take her chin in his hand then and turn her to face him. His eyes were still narrowed with residual anger.

"Don't you ever let that guy, or anybody else like him, touch you that way again. Do you hear me?" he growled.

"Okay," Breck squeaked. He seemed more than protective—almost possessive. But Breck chased the hope from her mind as she gazed up at him. He was just teaching her how to further take care of volatile situations in the future.

"Okay," he mumbled, releasing her. Then, shaking his head, he added, "I'm sick of this—" He paused and looked away before finishing, "—crap." Then with a heavy sigh, he said, "I'm going home, Breck. You can go too, if you'd like."

"Okay," she said. She'd seen him like this before

and imagined he was feeling the same way she was—that people were jerks, that the world was going to the dogs. And it only seemed to be getting worse. What happened to fidelity in marriage? To honesty in business? To family dinner around the table, children using their imaginations and playing outside instead of sitting in dark rooms watching television or having seizures caused by video game graphics?

Reese went into his office and retrieved some files from his desk. "Good night, Breck," he mumbled on his way out.

"Good night, sir," she called after him.

Collapsing in her chair, Breck let out a long breath of discouragement. What a day it had been! She couldn't remember the last time she'd experienced such a range of emotion in such a short period of time. From excitement about her birthday—delight over Reese's attention to it—to the bottom of the bog with anger, bitterness, and discouragement.

Closing her eyes for a moment, she remembered how good Reese had smelled that morning when he'd given her the sweater—how adorable his pride in his wrapping job was—how warm and strong his body felt under her palms as she had pushed him against the wall to keep him from beating the life out of Michael Allen. Gosh, he was fabulous! Secretly she liked that he could've and would've beat Michael Allen to a pulp. It seemed few people stood up for things (especially the honor and protection of women) anymore. Maybe they were too selfish—or too out of shape physically. Maybe they were scared of getting thrown in jail. Breck shook her head at how many cases she'd seen go through the office of good men who were facing lawsuits and jail because they'd manhandled some gang member that had bullied or beaten up their ten-year-old child. But what frightened her most was the thought that men like Reese were rare because the men of her day and age just didn't care.

Pulling out of her current thought process—for it was nothing but despairing—Breck gathered her things. She would leave work early because she wanted to enjoy her evening with her friends. And if she were going to, she needed a few hours peace and quiet to recapture her good mood. Home would do it. She'd run home, turn on some Harry Connick Jr., and have a piece of the pumpkin pie waiting in her fridge and maybe a short nap. That would help. Still, she wished Michael Allen had never shown up at the office. The idiot had cheated her out of three valuable hours spent in Reese's presence. Jerk.

CHAPTER THREE

Marcelli's seemed more exciting than usual that night. At least it seemed that way to Breck. The incident at the office with Mr. Allen had definitely dampened her spirits for a time. But after a nice long shower, some soothing music, and a little baking, Breck had felt quite revived. In fact, when she'd pulled on the beautiful pumpkin sweater Reese had given to her, she actually felt quite enchanted. Furthermore, the knowledge that Reese had inconvenienced his mother on her behalf—that he had wadded the sweater up, stuffed it in a fish-and-tackle store box, and wrapped it himself—it was too delightful! Wearing the sweater caused Breck to imagine being wrapped in Reese's arms—warm, secure. It was an incredible sensation and added to the bounce she had in her step as she entered Marcelli's with her friends to celebrate her birthday.

As Dean Martin sang "That's Amore" softly in the background, Breck and her friends ordered entrees, giggled, talked about life, and just generally had a wonderful evening. The atmosphere in the restaurant was especially perfect. Breck noted the lights were dimmer than usual. The delicious aromas of olive oil, garlic, and pasta blended perfectly with the low hum made by patrons in conversation, and Sherryl had arranged for their favorite waiter to attend their table that evening, allowing for more silly frivolity.

Later, as they waited for their desserts to be brought out, Breck relaxed against the back of her chair and sighed—content. Smiling, she quickly surveyed the scene before her.

There was Barb, laughing with merriment—Barb, who was married to the sweetest man—Barb, who had two sweet little toddler daughters only a year apart—Barb, who had spent two years before college leading troubled teens through the wilderness on survival treks. Breck shook her head, finding it hard to believe that this was the same woman who used to hunt and kill rattlesnakes for food. Now she was the vision of the perfect wife and mother and completely content about it.

Breck smiled again as she looked to Trixie, busily sculpting a rabbit out of the remains of her meat ravioli. Trixie was engaged now—to the man of her dreams, Bobby Jepson. She was quite the successful floral designer, and Breck was surprised she didn't sculpt more flora and fauna when they were out to eat. Trixie was the most patient person Breck had ever known, and she loved her for it.

Kay was a sweetheart! She'd been a forensic chemist in the days before she married. In fact, whenever Kay hosted a get-together at her house, she used large test tubes for punch glasses. And her home was completely covered in fabulous, handmade quilts! Kay could sew like the wind and anything she set her mind to. She was the crafty one of the bunch, and Breck admired her for it.

Now, Sherryl—Sherryl was the group clown. As Breck studied her for a moment—trying not to burst out into belly laughs as Kay snapped a picture of Sherryl with two straws hanging out of her nose— she wondered at how the woman kept up with herself! Sherryl seemed to have endless amounts of energy. And it was a good thing, for she was one of the best-known and most requested photographers in the city! Owning her own photography studio downtown, Sherryl kept a crazy schedule of portrait and product shoots. Still, with all the things that pulled her in every direction, she was careful to make time for her friends. Sherryl was dating a nice man—a landscaper—and Breck secretly hoped that wedded bliss would soon be the outcome.

As she sat studying and appreciating her good friends, Breck was too preoccupied to perceive the hush that fell over the patrons at Marcelli's in that moment. In fact, it wasn't until she noticed her friends all looking at her—smiles stretching from ear to ear— that she realized something was afoot.

"What?" she asked, glancing down at her beautiful pumpkin sweater. Had she spilled sauce on it?

She gasped as a black-gloved hand suddenly covered her mouth from behind. Next a man's voice— his breath hot on her neck—whispered in her ear, "Be still. The Highwayman of Tanglewood owns you now."

Breck recognized the phrase as one of her favorites from the book she so adored, *The Highwayman of Tanglewood*. However, she did not recognize the voice. The man's hand still covered her mouth tightly, but Breck could see the delight blazing across her friends' faces.

So this was what they were up to all week, she thought. They had hired someone to be her Highwayman of Tanglewood.

Breck tried to push the man's hand from her mouth so she could turn and see him. But he tightened his grip, coaxing her to rise from her seat as he whispered, "Do not struggle. I'll not harm you. I simply intend to have you." Whoever was playing the Highwayman was delivering his lines straight from the book and with perfection! As she stood, Breck began to giggle, for the expressions on her friends' faces were worth a lifetime of other expressions from other people. They were nothing short of entirely delighted with themselves!

Once she was standing, Breck felt the Highwayman's free arm encircle her waist from behind, pulling her back against his body. He bent, resting his chin on her shoulder for a moment before playfully nuzzling he neck.

"Come away with me, sweet Breck," the Highwayman whispered. By this time, every patron in Marcelli's large group dining area was staring at the scene. "What say you?" he added, removing his hand from her mouth and letting it rest at her throat.

Breck tried not to giggle, but it was all entirely too wonderful! A little more public than she would've perhaps preferred, but wonderful all the same.

"I say, who are you Highwayman?" she asked, quoting the book.

"Ah! But that you should know, sweet Breck," the man whispered.

At that point, the thought flittered through Breck's mind, *How perfect if you were Reese Thatcher!* Knowing that to be impossible, however, Breck began to wrack her brain for other possibilities.

Slowly, Breck began to turn in the man's arms in order to better view the secreted Highwayman of Tanglewood. But suddenly, the lighting in the room burned even more dimly—someone having turned them down. Still, enraptured by the entire event, Breck smiled as she saw she was standing in the arms of a man dressed head to toe in black. A large, draping cowl hung down over his already masked eyes and nose; a flowing cape drooped from his shoulders reaching nearly to the floor. Breck looked down to see that he was indeed wearing black breeches and black boots that cuffed just below his knee. Reaching out, she took the silky fabric of his shirt in her hand, unable to believe the perfect detail of his costume. She could hear the repeat of Sherryl's digital camera shutter clicking away at a mad pace as she tried to imagine who would be willing to involve himself in such an outlandish scheme. The light was too dim and Breck was held too closely in the Highwayman's arms to get a good look at him. Still, his mouth was easily seen. She tried to recognize the grin he wore, but his mustache and goatee hid even the shape of his lips well.

Sherryl was on her feet now, her camera shutter wearing itself out with her maniacal snapping. Breck reached out, running her hands caressively the breadth of the Highwayman's shoulders. Two could play at this game, and her friends deserved a good show for all their trouble.

"I know you not, sir," Breck said in a whisper. "Surely I would remember such a shape of a man." The Highwayman's grin broadened at her quoted banter.

"Indeed, would you?" he asked. Breck was certain he was doing more to disguise his voice than the simple method of speaking in a whisper, for she didn't recognize it at all.

"I would, sir," she answered.

"And the taste of his kiss, my sweet?" the Highwayman whispered. "Would you surely remember such a taste of a kiss?"

Breck giggled. She couldn't take it any longer. "Who are you?" she begged.

The Highwayman paused in answering—probably to allow her friends to stop laughing for a moment.

"It matters to you?" he asked, using another line direct from the book.

"You're good, whoever you are," Breck said, smiling. She wondered if the girls had pooled their money and hired a professional stage actor to portray her dreamy Highwayman.

"I will reveal myself to you," he whispered, pulling her body tightly against his own, "on one condition." He'd strayed from the book's text now, and Breck giggled with delight.

"What's that?" she asked.

"The promise of a kiss," he whispered even more quietly. Breck's eyebrows rose in astonishment, and she looked back to her friends as they joined the other restaurant patrons in an encouraging applause.

"I don't kiss strangers," Breck countered. She was enjoying the playful event, but kissing someone she didn't know would be a bit over the edge.

"I am no stranger. It is well you know me," he whispered, again quoting the book.

She looked over to Sherryl, who paused in her mad photo taking long enough to say, "You do know him."

"We promised him you'd kiss him too, Breck," Barb called from her seat at the table.

"What?" Breck exclaimed, spinning around to face her traitorous friends.

"You know him, Breck. I promise," Kay assured her. Kay wouldn't deceive her about something like this—Breck knew that.

Turning back to face the Highwayman, Breck studied him again. Was he as tall as Reese Thatcher? She measured every man's height against Reese Thatcher's. She fancied that he was perhaps even taller—and then it hit her!

"Marty Sprague!" she exclaimed. "You little devil!"

Then turning to her friends, "How did you ever talk him into this?"

"You're sure you know who it is?" Trixie asked, giggling.

"Who else could it be?" Breck said. "Look how tall he is. It's Marty."

"Then…I'll get my kiss if I undress…uh…reveal my identity?" the Highwayman asked, still using his disguised voice.

Breck sighed, trying not to appear too disappointed. Marty was a sweet man, and how kind of him to be willing to go to such lengths to embarrass and delight her on her birthday. Would one kiss really be so bad? The only thing that worried her was the question of whether Marty would understand that a kiss between them would be a one-time "thank you" sort of kiss—not something to raise his hopes of anything more being possible. Still, how sweet he was to do this for her. Therefore, Breck relented.

"Okay," she said, causing her friends and the other restaurant patrons, waiters, and waitresses to cheer. Putting her arms around his neck to finally return his embrace, she said, "Reveal your identity, Highwayman of Tanglewood…and I agree to a kiss between us."

The Highwayman's smile broadened, and Breck felt her brows pucker in a frown. For as his grin grew into a smile revealing a nice set of pearly whites, Breck did not recognize it as Marty's. In fact, as he then began to tug on the well-made—however, false—mustache and goatee, Breck drew in her breath.

"It can't be!" she heard herself whisper.

But when the man then reached up, pulling back the cowl that draped his head and the mask that hid his eyes, Breck's knees gave way beneath her.

"Mr. Thatcher?" she breathed, and his arms banded around her tightly to keep her from slipping to the floor on rubbery knees.

"Now, Breck...surely you can be more familiar than that," Reese Thatcher chuckled. "Especially considering that we're about to become far more familiar than we've ever been before."

Breck felt dizzy for a moment—afraid she might pass out. Reese Thatcher? It couldn't be! Quickly she glanced to Sherryl—still wildly recording the event with her camera.

"We told you that you knew him," Sherryl giggled.

"B-but..." Breck stammered as she looked back to Reese. His smile was that of triumph. He knew she was rattled.

"Hey," he began, "I kept my end of the bargain and revealed myself. Now you need to keep yours."

Breck felt her eyes widen. Her side of the bargain? A kiss? She couldn't possibly!

Shaking her head—still in awed disbelief that it was Reese Thatcher who stood before her, Reese Thatcher holding her tightly in his arms, Reese Thatcher who had quoted lines to her from her favorite book—she whispered, "You're kidding, right?"

Reese chuckled. "No," came his monosyllabic answer.

"But…but…." Breck stammered.

"Kiss him, for Pete's sake, Breck," Barb demanded. "The man deserves at least that."

Standing there wrapped in Reese Thatcher's powerful arms—the restaurant patrons softly chanting, "Kiss him! Kiss him!" in unison—Breck felt her hands press against Reese's solid chest as his face moved closer to hers.

"I can't possibly," she told him.

He chuckled. "You have to," he told her. "They promised me."

"We did," Sherryl confirmed between shutter releases.

"Here," Reese said, turning Breck around so that her back pressed against the nearby wall. Then taking her face in his hands for a moment, he added, "Relax, Breck. It's just me."

Breck release a short, nervous giggle. Was he kidding? But in the next moment, she knew he wasn't.

His hands moved to encircle her neck—then one of his gloved thumbs moved slowly across her lips.

"Hold up," he mumbled, releasing her, stripping off his gloves, and letting them fall to the floor. Then his hands encircled her neck once more. His palms were warm—hot on her skin. And when his thumb caressed her lips again, slowly traveling from one side of her mouth to the other—as if preparing a canvas for the first stroke of a painter's masterpiece—Breck again thought she might literally pass out. His touch was incredible! It sent goose bumps erupting over her body—butterflies bursting forth from cocoons in her stomach! Just from his touch! If his simple touch had such an effect on her, Breck wondered if she could manage to live through a kiss from him. Could a woman drop dead of euphoria?

Instinctively, her hands gripped his strong forearms as his head descended toward hers.

"Mr. Thatcher, wait. I-I..." she whispered in an attempt to stall him. She truly wasn't certain she could remain conscious if he kissed her.

"It's Reese, Breck," he whispered a moment before his lips began to toy with her own.

Reese kissed her lightly at first—kissing first her upper lip and then her lower lip twice in succession.

"Oh my heck," Breck heard herself whisper. She heard Reese's low chuckle.

"Can I have my kiss now?" he asked.

"Well, yeah. But wasn't that—" Breck began. But before Breck could finish her sentence, Reese's lips took her own in a warm, powerful, driven kiss. And it wasn't a short peck of a kiss either! It endured on and on— deepened—warm, moist, and euphoric. Breck was instantly lost in it, returning the kiss as bravely as her shy twenty-one-year-old self could involve herself in a public kiss—with her boss!

Showers of wild, bright color exploded in her mind. Her heart seemed to skip several beats—her hands and feet going numb. And all from one kiss! She wasn't even aware of the cheering by restaurant patrons—for the roaring in her ears drowned out any noise. She didn't notice the super-fast snapping of

Sherryl's camera shutter or the waitress that dropped a tray nearby—stunned at what was happening in her place of employment.

Reese paused for a moment in administering the driven kiss—again kissing Breck's upper lip once and then her lower lip twice. He smiled down at her for a moment—an expression of understanding evident in his bluest of blue eyes. Then he kissed her again, and she nearly melted in a puddle at his feet as the heated moisture of his mouth mingled with her own.

Their kiss ended far too soon, and Reese helped Breck to stand as the restaurant patrons cheered and whistled with delight.

"And now," he said, bending to retrieve his gloves from the floor. "I must go…before your father catches me and has me sent to the gallows for threatening his daughter's virtue." Gently he took her chin in his hand once more. "Happy birthday, Breck." He left then among the applause of the restaurant patrons and staff.

Breck's knees wouldn't support her any longer, and she slid down the wall into a sitting position on the restaurant floor.

"Oh my heck, you guys!" she breathed as her dearest friends gathered around her—delighted eyes aflame with mischief!

"Are we the greatest or what?" Kay giggled.

Barb and Trixie each offered a hand to Breck, and she accepted their help—grateful for the needed support to stand.

"I don't know whether to hug you guys or kill you!" Breck giggled as she began to regain her composure.

"Oh my heck! You've even got five-o'clock-shadow rash on your cheek!" Trixie squealed, having noticed the slight pink rash left on Breck's cheek as a result of Reese Thatcher's attention.

Breck buried her face in her hands, uncertain whether to take flight in the blissful memory of Reese's kiss or drop in a dead faint at the thought of having to face him at work come Monday morning.

"I say we blow this joint and head for my darkroom!" Sherryl said, waving her camera over her head.

"Yeah, yeah, yeah!" Barb agreed. "Don't you want to relive the moment through the magic of photography, Breck?"

Everyone hugged and giggled, and Breck could not ignore the delicious thrill running through her veins. Reese Thatcher had kissed her! It was her wildest dream come true! And it had been nothing but pure ambrosia. How could she ever be the same? She wouldn't—and she knew it. She knew that at some point, her heart would come tumbling down from the emotional flight it was on in those moments—but she would worry about that later. For now, all she wanted to do was live Reese's kisses over and over and over again in her mind. She hoped Sherryl's camera had captured a moment or two of their kissing on the memory card. How perfect to be able to look at their kiss—to verify to her mind that it actually had happened—that it hadn't been just a perfect dream.

Reese Thatcher chuckled as he wadded the cape, cowl, and mask into a ball, tossing them on the seat beside him. The look on Breck's face when he'd unmasked had been priceless! Utterly priceless! For a moment she'd looked like she would faint dead in her tracks. He'd never forget the way her eyes widened, how the blush rose to her cheeks when she realized it was her boss dressed up like an idiot. Her friends may have been silly, absolutely crazy, but she was lucky to have them. You had to love someone a lot to go to such lengths on their behalf. He envied Breck for having such good people in her life.

Reese had good people in his life too. But at that moment he realized how distant they had become—how distant he had caused them to become—and he felt deep regret. Still, he wouldn't think about it. Instead, he chuckled again at the memory of the look on Breck's face when she'd realized who he was. And he thought about her sweet kiss—how good she tasted—how soft her skin was—the vanilla fragrance of it. He thought how beautiful she looked in his mother's pumpkin sweater and was flattered that she'd been wearing it.

He hadn't been surprised he'd enjoyed kissing her so much—for he'd known he would beforehand. It was the fact that he'd almost not been able to find the self-control to stop kissing her when he did. He could've kissed her all night. Maybe it had been far too passionate a kiss for their first one, but he hadn't been able to help himself. She was just as delicious as he'd thought she'd be. More so! He shook his head, realizing that facing her at work—keeping his hands off her at work—would be all the more difficult now.

Still, he was glad he'd poked his head out of his shell long enough to be involved in Breck's friends' crazy scheming. Because that little trinket he called his assistant was getting under his skin, and he had to try to quench the thirst for her that had been building in him from the moment he hired her.

Pushing the clutch in, he started his pickup, shifted into first, and left Marcelli's parking lot with a smile and a desire in his heart to be a better man. Picking up his cell, he dialed.

"Hello?" came the sweet, beloved voice on the other end.

"Hi, Mom. You'll never guess what I've been up to tonight," he began.

❦

"One-hour photo be hanged!" Sherryl announced as she exited the darkroom. Sherryl was obsessive enough about her hobby-slash-profession that she always kept high-end photo editing computers and printers at home too. And tonight, Sherryl's talents were really going to pay off for Breck.

"Look at this puppy!" she exclaimed. "Straight off the cover of *Romantic Times*." Sherryl held up an eleven-by-fourteen enlargement, and a hot blush rose to Breck's cheeks as she looked at the picture.

"Whoa, baby! Look at that kiss!" Kay giggled.

And sure enough, there—nearly as large as life— was the perfect and tangible evidence of the fact that

Reese Thatcher had indeed kissed Breck that evening at Marcelli's. A delightful shiver broke over Breck's entire body as she stared at the photo. As always, Sherryl had managed to catch the perfect moment. Her artist's eye and camera shutter had captured a moment of light in the universe—the moment when Reese's slightly parted lips had just touched Breck's—the split second before he'd pressed his mouth firmly to her own. It made for quite the intimate and thrilling photograph.

"This has to be the best kissing picture I've ever shot, Breck," the skinny blonde said. She added, "I'll have to do a sixteen-by-twenty...for your bedroom too. Mounted with a red matte, it will be perfect."

"Do we all get copies?" Trixie asked.

"I want mine with a red matte too...only eight-by-ten will be fine," Barb added.

"Done deal," Sherryl said.

Breck put her hands to her blazing-hot cheeks. "You guys are crazy. How am I ever going to face him at work on Monday?"

The women erupted into laughter as they looked to their friend.

"Who cares!" Kay exclaimed. "He was good!"

Breck blushed more deeply and smiled, shaking her head. "You guys are awful."

"No, seriously, Breck," Barb said. "It looked good. Was it as good a kiss as it looked...as good as it looks in the photo?"

Breck sighed, still light-headed from the experience. "Better," she said.

"He is so hot, Breck!" Trixie reminded them all, as if they needed reminding. "You have to have him."

"What?" Breck gasped, giggling. "You do realize he's Reese Thatcher, right?"

"Oh, honey," Kay said. "Believe me...we realize." Then she smiled and pointed to the picture, to Reese's parted lips. "Look at that kiss! Look at that man! How did you not drop dead on the spot?"

Breck shook her head as her arms and legs covered themselves in goose bumps at the sight of the photograph before her.

"I do *not* know," Breck answered honestly.

Late that night, as Breck sat on the sofa in her apartment—comfortable in her flannel pumpkin-patterned pajamas and a mug of hot chocolate to relax her—she gazed at the picture Sherryl had given her of their kiss—hers and Reese's. She couldn't believe he'd done it—dressed up like some idiot, run into a very popular, very populated restaurant, and played her Highwayman! It was unbelievable. As unbelievable as the kiss he'd taken—given—shared with her. Again those imaginary butterflies that lie dormant in every woman's stomach waiting for the right man burst into flight, causing her to shiver. She tried to enjoy the memory of that wonderful kiss—the taste of it— the feel of his mouth to hers, his hands on her skin. But the knowledge of having to face him at work on Monday was drilling its way into her mind. Still, any man chivalrous enough to play the Highwayman of Tanglewood in public—surely he'd be chivalrous enough to realize how hard it would be for her to face him on Monday.

Taking a sip of the warm, sweet liquid from the mug in her hands, Breck closed her eyes and remembered how handsome—how absolutely gorgeous—Reese had been dressed in the period clothing of an aristocratic highwayman. If she concentrated very hard, she could still feel his thumb caress her lips—smell the aftershave on his cheek. What a perfect, fabulous night it had been. She would try to keep it in her dreams all weekend and worry about Monday morning on Monday morning.

CHAPTER FOUR

Breck spent Saturday and Sunday vacillating between euphoria and an anticipatory anxiety. Each time she looked at the pictures Sherryl had taken at Marcelli's—especially the one of the moment Reese's lips first touched her own—goose bumps, butterflies, and delightful shivers of every kind traveled through her body. It was truly a dream moment! And yet, whenever she thought of having to face Reese at work on Monday, she felt nervous, anxious, nauseated. Still, she knew he had made great sacrifices on her behalf. And there was the matter of the sweater he'd had his mother knit, as well. A major thank you was in order. And unable to think of anything else more appropriate, Breck arrived at work on Monday morning with one of her famous, and very delectable, homemade pumpkin pies in hand.

If there was one thing she'd noticed about Reese over the past six months as his assistant, it was that he had a huge weakness where baked goods were concerned. Anytime anyone brought homemade cookies, cakes, or pies to the office for any reason, Reese was always first in line to taste them. Therefore, Breck had put her faith in her pumpkin pie as being an apropos thank you for her pumpkin sweater. She'd worked for years—ever since she started baking as a young girl—to perfect her pumpkin pie filling recipe. And although she might not be very confident in other aspects of her life, she knew her pumpkin pie was a winner. She'd won first place at the Colorado State Fair seven years running with it.

As far as thanking Reese for the scene at Marcelli's—well, the pie would have to serve for that as well. The pie accompanied by verbal thanks, that was.

So with pumpkin pie in hand, Breck stepped off the elevator that crisp autumn Monday morning and smiled as Patty greeted her with a friendly wave.

"Hey there, Breck," Patty said, smiling. "What are you toting in this morning?"

"Something for Mr. Thatcher," Breck answered, adding, "and a thank you note for you." Balancing the pie carefully in one hand, Breck reached into her coat pocket and retrieved the thank you note she'd written for Patty regarding the lovely autumn snow globe she had gifted her.

"Oh, how sweet, Breck," Patty chimed. "You're so thoughtful."

"You're the thoughtful one, Patty," Breck told her. Then looking around quickly, she asked, "Is Mr. Thatcher in yet this morning, do you know?"

Patty shook her head and shrugged her shoulders. "Haven't seen him."

"Thanks," Breck said with relief. She wanted to

get to her desk before he arrived—try to gather her composure.

But her plans to prepare herself to face him were thrown to the wind. For as she rounded the corner to her desk, she saw him standing in his office door, fiddling with his cell phone.

There was absolutely no way to avoid him. And so, drawing in a deep breath and trying to find an ounce of courage and composure, she walked directly to her desk.

"Good morning, Breck," Reese greeted with a knowing grin as she set the pie on her desk and began to remove her coat.

"Good morning, Mr. Thatcher," she said, unable to look at him and trying to sound nonchalant.

She heard him chuckle. "Oh, surely we're beyond 'Mr. Thatcher,' by now, Breck," he said. "Especially after the other night at—"

"You're right," she interrupted, a crimson blush already blazing on her cheeks. "And speaking of the other day," she began, "I owe you a truckload of thank-yous." Finally, she found the nerve to look at him and then wished she wouldn't have. He was too gorgeous—too knowing when it came to her discomfort! And what he was wearing was not only a bit different from what he normally wore to work but absolutely perfect on him! He often wore jeans to work, his profession and need to remain inconspicuous allowing for a more casual manner of dress. However, this day his jeans were adorably worn out! In fact, as he turned to remove a yellow sticky note someone had left on his office door, Breck noticed the dime-sized holes that were evident at the corner of each of the pockets on the seat of his pants.

For Pete's sake! she thought. She could see his underwear peeking through the holes—his white underwear! A raggedy, old blue-black baseball cap was partially shoved in one pocket too.

Complementing the rather intriguing holes in the rear end of his jeans were a pair of beat up, weathered, nearly ragged, black Roper boots Reese wore. And his shirt? Good grief! His shirt was nothing but a tight-fitting, red, rather faded, sort of misshapen T-shirt. He was absolutely drop-dead gorgeous!

"You do?" Reese asked, causing Breck to close her gaping mouth and frantically try to remember what she'd said before his adorable appearance had so completely distracted her.

"I do what?" she asked, unable to organize her thoughts.

He chuckled. "You said you owe me a truckload of thank-yous."

"Oh, yeah!" she said, nervous and giggling. "I do!"

With his familiar mischievous grin spreading across his face, Reese walked closer to Breck until he stood exactly in front of her.

Breck looked up into his face as he said, "Well?"

She was undone! How could she possibly ever remain calm in his presence again? Her eyes lingered on his delicious mouth, and she was reminded that she knew just how delicious it was.

"Well what?" she breathed.

Again Reese chuckled. "Is that pie plate on your desk my thank-you?"

The pie! Of course!

"Oh. Yes! It is," Breck exclaimed, turning from him and retrieving the pie from her desk. Holding the pie out to him, she said, "I hope you like pumpkin. I thought it appropriate, considering the beautiful sweater your mother made and all."

"Mmmm!" he hummed, removing the aluminum foil from the pie and inhaling of its mouth-watering fragrance. "Pumpkin pie is my absolute favorite," he told her.

"Oh! I'm glad," Breck said, swallowing hard. "Well then...I hope you enjoy it and—"

"So this is what I get for the pumpkin sweater?" he said, smiling at her.

"Yes. I hope it's okay. The sweater is beautiful. I know a pie doesn't really compare and—"

"What do I get for the thing at Marcelli's then?" he interrupted.

Breck felt goose bumps prickle at the back of her neck and on her legs. "I-I was thinking that...maybe the pie would do," she stammered.

He laughed wholeheartedly for a moment. Then winking at her and cupping her face in one strong hand for a moment, he said, "I'm just teasing you, Breck." Breck sighed with relief, but it was short-lived. "I was hoping for some copies of those pictures your friend took though." He smiled. "What do you think?"

"Oh. The pictures," Breck stammered. "Of course. I'll have her make some copies for you. I mean, your costume was incredible and—"

"It was fun, huh?" he said, lowering his voice. Breck looked up to find his eyes twinkling—bright with amusement at the memory.

"Fun?" she breathed. "Oh, yes. Yes it was...fun."

"We'll have to do it again sometime," he whispered in a low, very provocative tone.

"We will?" Breck choked. Reese chuckled and turned to leave her, intent on his office.

"Thanks for the pie, Breck," he called to her a moment before he shut his door.

Once Reese's office door was shut, Breck collapsed into her desk chair, trying to take in a deep breath. He was unbelievable! She'd almost grabbed the front of his T-shirt and pulled his head down toward hers to kiss him!

Fanning herself with one hand—trying to ease the temperature increase Reese had caused in her—Breck adjusted her headset just in time to answer the phone.

"Wilson Investigation, Reese Thatcher's office. May I help you?" she answered. The voice on the other line dispelled her euphoria.

"Miss McCall? This is Danielle Allen. Is Mr. Thatcher available to take my call?" the sobbing woman asked.

"Oh, Mrs. Allen," Breck stammered. "Let me see

if he's in." Placing Mrs. Allen on hold, Breck beeped Reese's phone.

"Breck?" he answered.

"Mrs. Allen is on line one, Mr. Thatcher. She sounds very upset," she explained.

"I'll take the call. Thanks," he said. The teasing tone that had been in his voice only moments before was completely dissipated.

Breck resisted the urge to break company policy and eavesdrop on the conversation. Still, the thought of poor Mrs. Allen pinched her heart. Michael Allen was a jerk! And that was putting it mildly. Every time Reese was handed a case where one or the other member of a married couple was being unfaithful, she felt physically sick. What was wrong with people? Especially someone like Michael Allen. Danielle Allen was beautiful! Not only to look at, but she was a wonderful person. And their baby was adorable. What was wrong with that man? Secretly she wished she'd let Reese beat some sense into him the other day. But she knew that would've only landed Reese in trouble with some sort of wiener-spun lawsuit pending. Still, it made her angry. It hurt her heart.

A few minutes later, Reese opened his office door and stuck his head out, looking to Breck.

"Hey, Breck," he said. It was obvious he was infuriated. "Get me Lowel down at Stevens and Rodham, will you?"

"Sure," Breck agreed.

"Patch it in as a conference call on line one, please," he further instructed.

"Of course," she said.

❦

Breck spent the next two hours pulling stuff out of the Allen file and getting it ready to take over to Mrs. Allen's attorney. The more she worked on it, the more angry she became—the more discouraged. By the time her break rolled around, she felt like she'd been through an entire week of work. Her disposition wasn't very friendly at that moment, so she decided to just sit back in her chair and read the comics in the newspaper Reese always deposited on her desk when he was finished with it every morning. Something lighthearted—that's what she needed.

She'd almost finished the comic page of the newspaper and was just swallowing the last bite of her honey-roasted peanuts package when the door to Reese's office opened and he stepped out.

"There's something you should know, Breck," he said, striding to where she sat.

"There is?" she asked, wondering what in the world he was going to tell her. Was there more drama with the Allen case?

She was suddenly quite self-conscious and uncomfortable when he hunkered down next to her and took one of her hands between his own.

"Breck," Reese began. Breck could hardly breathe! Had Mrs. Allen taken matters into her own hands? Had she lost it and...and...

"That is…by far…the best pumpkin pie I have ever eaten," he said. There was no hint of teasing or amusement in his expression. But still, Breck thought, *He can't be serious.*

"Pardon?" Breck breathed.

Reese shook his head and inhaled deeply. "I never thought I'd say this to any woman," he began, "and part of me feels like a traitor even thinking this. But… but, Breck…" Breck waited for him to finish, unable to breathe or believe what he was saying. "That pie was better than my *mother's*!"

Breck let out a relieved sigh. What a kidder he was!

"Oh, oh sure," she giggled. He had her going for a moment. "I hope you enjoyed it all the same, Mr. Thatcher."

She was astonished, however, when he suddenly took her chin firmly in his hand, nearly glared at her, and said, "No. I'm serious."

There was not a hint of sarcasm in his voice or expression. Breck realized he was actually sincere in the compliment.

"Really?" was all she could say—a delighted smile spreading across her face. "Well, I'm glad you like it." She giggled a little, for he seemed unsettled.

"Do you realize what this means?" he asked, shaking his head.

"No. What?" Breck coaxed.

He stared at her for a moment, seeming to study her face with too much intensity to leave her comfortable. Then he stood up and simply said, "I've got to run over to Stevens and Rodham. Will you just forward my calls to my voicemail?" And he was gone.

Breck sat in her chair, completely perplexed. His behavior had been so odd—as if finding a pie that was better than his mother's was somehow life-altering. Still, she giggled, for his strange behavior had, once again, lightened her heavy heart.

Tucking the newspaper away in the recycle bin, she managed to get her headset on just as the phone rang.

"Wilson Investigation, Reese Thatcher's office. May I help you?"

Reese climbed into his pickup and laid his head on the steering wheel for a moment. He was in trouble! All weekend long he'd done nothing but obsess about what had transpired between him and Breck at Marcelli's on Friday night. Well, he'd worked on stripping his deck, gone to the game with Bill, and watched some Bruce Willis movie on TV. But mostly he'd had trouble getting the taste of that kiss with Breck out of his mind. And now this! No one—absolutely no one— made a better pumpkin pie than his mother! He was a bit unnerved that something so seemingly miniscule could throw him for such a big loop. The pie Breck had baked for him as thanks for "the sweater," as she put it, was absolutely the best he'd ever had. And there was no reason on earth that a man's office girl should bake a better pumpkin pie than his mother!

Maybe he'd just been deprived of pumpkin pie for too long. Maybe he'd just been really, really hungry, having skipped breakfast that morning. But he shook his head as he clutched and turned the key in his pickup ignition. This girl was getting under his skin—and long before the whole fiasco he'd involved himself in at Marcelli's—long before she'd made a better pumpkin pie than his own mother. Breck McCall was dangerous to the order of the life Reese Thatcher had chosen. She made him think of hazardous things like home, his cute little nieces, his ol' cow Honey—the last he'd raised at home before he'd left for the city and a big-city career.

He closed his eyes, trying to block out the image of Breck in that dang pumpkin sweater his mother had knitted. Tried not to remember how she'd melted in his arms when he'd kissed her—how delicious that kiss tasted.

Shifting into first, he peeled out of the parking lot. He'd drive around a bit. That would clear his head. Maybe he'd call his mother and ask if she thought ol' Honey would make it through the winter. He wouldn't tell her that he'd met a girl that made a better pumpkin pie than she did.

CHAPTER FIVE

Lunch with Patty had been unexpectedly soothing. Breck was amazed at Patty's ability to calm her down, help her remember the good in the world.

"Not everybody marries a jerk, Breck," Patty told her. They'd been discussing the Allens' situation. "Look at me and my Joe, for example. Twenty-five years of wedded bliss...and I mean it!" Yes, Breck enjoyed Patty's company, her positive attitude toward life, her hope in humanity.

However, when she returned from lunch and rounded the corner of the office to find Jamie Reynolds standing by her desk talking with another office girl, Breck felt her optimistic mood begin to evaporate again. One thing would sour a day faster than Michael Allen—and that was Jamie Reynolds.

Jamie worked in filing. She was a sharp-tongued, trouble-making "hoochie"—as Barb would call her—with the reddest of red hair and the most hateful green eyes Breck had ever seen. She was quite curvaceous and liked to remind everyone of it by wearing clothes that were far too tight and revealing. In actuality, Breck was surprised that old Mr. Wilson kept her on. She often wondered what blackmail material Jamie had cached away on Mr. Wilson, for she made everyone's life miserable. Furthermore, she was forever going on about which man at the office was pursuing her on any given day of the week. For some reason, however, she'd stayed clear of trying to link herself up with Reese through the gossip line. Breck thought this was because even a woman as ignorant as Jamie Reynolds knew no one would believe Reese Thatcher would consort with a woman like her.

As Breck approached her desk, she thought about how completely she hated having to feign friendliness to Jamie. But Jamie was the kind of girl that would chew you up and spit you out if you rubbed her the wrong way. Still, Breck loathed dealing with her—and it was obvious she would have to.

"Well, I've had it!" Jamie said in a lowered voice to the girl she had cornered. As Breck approached, she heard her add, "Someone needs to take him down a size or two, and I'm ready to do it."

Breck felt the hair on the back of her neck prickle, sensing something very bad was about to happen.

"What do you mean?" Breck sighed. First of all, she couldn't believe that Jamie was talking trash about someone while standing in her office. The girl knew Breck didn't like to hear all her dirty laundry.

"Your boss! That's what I mean!" Jamie exclaimed, raising her voice a bit. The girl who Jamie had been talking to before Breck arrived rolled her eyes at Breck as she made some sad excuse to leave Breck to the wolf.

"Mr. Thatcher?" Breck asked, a strange, nauseated sensation flooding her stomach. This was not good. Breck knew it.

"Surely you've noticed how arrogant and superior he acts," Jamie whispered. "Walking around with his nose in the air, never giving anyone the time of day. It's time he learned people deserve more respect. I'm gonna slap him hard with sexual harassment. We'll see how high and mighty he is then."

"What?" Breck exclaimed. What kind of an idiot would tell her—Reese's assistant—about plans to accuse him? Still, she thought it might be wise to feign the ally for a moment longer. At least until she knew more about what Jamie intended to do. "Reese Thatcher is the only gentleman around here," Breck growled.

"Exactly," Jamie sneered. "Or so he claims. Today I caught him looking dead at my chest...and don't tell me he wasn't checking me out."

Breck frowned and shook her head as she glanced down at the plunging neckline of Jamie's blouse—not to mention the two strategically placed, hot pink daisies glaring at her from each breast.

"Anybody is gonna look at that shirt, Jamie." Realizing this was exactly Jamie's intention, she added, "But I guess that was the plan."

Jamie glared at Breck. "You *would* defend him. I should've expected that you were too wowed by his good looks to see through him for what he really is."

Breck clenched her teeth tightly for a moment,

trying to find the self-control to simply walk away. However, she couldn't. She was sick of women like Jamie—and the world seemed to have too many of them. It was time someone took one down.

"Jamie…it is so way obvious that you're just ticked off because Reese doesn't give you the time of day. And believe me, you try to accuse him of anything…and I'll make this conversation public knowledge."

Before Breck could even fathom what was to come, she felt the hot sting of a hard slap against her right cheek. Putting her hand quickly to her throbbing face, Breck looked back to Jamie in time to see (but not avoid) the painful slap across her other cheek. Jamie had paused just long enough between slaps to turn her chunky silver ring so that the gems were on the inside of her hand. In doing so she had assured that the second slap left a painful and now bleeding cut on Breck's left cheekbone.

Breck stood stunned—unable to believe the viciousness of the woman's attack. "You're crazy!" she exclaimed.

"Well, you're naive," Jamie told her. "No…you're plain stupid." She turned to leave but paused, turning back to Breck. Waving an index finger at her, she whispered, "You're an idiot if you think he's going to ever give you the time of day. And you're even dumber if you think Wilson won't pay me off when I charge him."

Breck pressed her wound with her fingers and then looked at the blood it left on them—still awed by what had happened. She was going to say something, even though she didn't know what, but when Dave Pullman rounded the corner, she decided to keep quiet. There was nothing she could say anyway.

As Jamie turned to leave again, she paused as she saw Dave and heard Reese's office door open.

"What's going on here?" Reese asked, perplexed. Patty appeared almost instantly, and Breck breathed a sigh of relief as she realized that Patty must've heard or seen something and called security.

"Tell him what's going on, Jamie," Patty urged. She glared at Jamie, folding her arms across her chest in a gesture of waiting for the woman's response.

"What do you mean?" Jamie asked, feigning ignorance. "We were just talking."

Reese looked to Breck, his frown deepening as he strode to where she stood. Taking her chin none too gently in his hand, he tipped her head and looked at the bleeding cut on her cheek.

"What're you doing, Jamie?" he growled.

"She's assaulting Breck, that's what she's doing," Patty said, "and planning to slap you with a sexual harassment charge too," she added.

Again Breck was thankful that Patty was always running to someone's assistance. She must've been in the hallway just outside Reese's office—heard the conversation prior to Jamie's violence and called security and Reese.

Reese nodded as he glared at Jamie, "Oh, I see," he mumbled. "Dave," he said, releasing Breck's face for a moment, reaching down, taking a tissue from the box on her desk, and holding it to her cheek.

"Yes, sir?" Dave nodded.

"You wanna take Miss Hellfire here to her desk, let her get *only* her personal items, and then escort her out of the building, please?" Reese ordered.

"My pleasure, sir," Dave answered.

"You can't fire me!" Jamie argued. "She hit me first!" she lied.

"She hit you first?" Reese shouted, enraged by the obvious lie. Reese took Breck's hand and placed the tissue in it as he turned toward Jamie. But Breck read the look on his face and knew if she let him continue toward the woman in his state of mind that he'd be facing an assault charge in the least.

"Dave," Breck said, calmly stepping between Reese and Jamie.

"Follow me, Miss Reynolds," Dave said, taking her arm carefully and directing her away from the scene.

"You haven't seen the last of me, Reese Thatcher!" Jamie shouted as everyone in the office began poking their heads out of office and cubicle spaces to see what all the commotion was about.

"You got that right!" Reese hollered after her. "You seem to have forgotten there's a security camera watching this space. We'll see who gets charged with what."

Patty took hold of Reese's arm. "Settle down, Reese. Settle down," she soothed. "She'll get hers."

Reese sighed heavily, trying to gain control of his

temper. Then he turned his attention to Breck once more.

"Let me see," he said, pulling her hand away from the cut. He took her chin in his hand again and inspected the injury more closely. Then he turned her face to look at the other cheek. "Look at the welt she left here!" he growled. "Patty, have Dave get that security tape copied, please," he said to Patty, although still looking at Breck's face. "Breck," he said then, releasing his hold on her face, "can I see you in my office?" It was a command under the guise of a polite question, and Breck's heart began to hammer with anxiety. Would he be angry with her as well? Would Dave be escorting her from the building in the next few minutes?

Reese opened the door to his office and stood aside, motioning for Breck to enter first. Closing the door behind them, he said, "I am so sorry, Breck."

His apology was not only unnecessary but unexpected as well.

"Pardon me?" Breck said, uncertain whether she had heard him correctly.

"You shouldn't have to come to work and worry about whether or not you're going to end up in the hospital by the end of the day," he explained, taking her chin in his hand again. He studied the wound on her cheek, and Breck knew he must've tugged at it a bit because a sharp pain stung her there for a moment. "Yep," he muttered, releasing her chin. "You need a stitch or two."

"Really?" Breck gasped, going to the nearby wall

mirror. As she studied the small but deep cut on her cheek, she felt tears welling up in her eyes. Suddenly, what had just happened with Jamie—the thoughts of poor Mrs. Allen—all the ugliness of the day—washed over her like a hot, horrible rain.

"Why are people so awful?" she cried, burying her face in her hands for a moment, unable to stop her tears. Her heart actually hurt because of the cruelty in her day, and she felt like she wanted to curl up and hide away from the world. She was angry too and looked up at Reese as everything she was feeling began spilling from her lips.

"Mrs. Allen is a good, kind, beautiful woman! How can her husband be such a creep? And that cute little baby. How can he not appreciate what he has…or rather had?" she corrected.

"I don't know," Reese mumbled, shrugging his shoulders.

But Breck's mind and mouth were bent on venting. "And Jamie," she continued. "She's just ticked off because you won't give her the time of day. So she decides to slap you with a sexual harassment suit?" Breck frowned and shook her head, still unable to believe what had just happened outside Reese's office. "I mean…you're the least harassing man I've ever met in my life! Did she really think she could make that stick? Well, in today's world…she probably could've! And to sink so low as to wear something so tacky as that stupid blouse with two big pink daisies smack on her…on her…bosoms!" By this time Breck was pacing back and forth in front of Reese as she rambled. He just watched her go back and forth, back and forth, like a spectator at a tennis match, as she raved on.

"I mean, who wouldn't look at her chest? I did! I mean, what happened to decency? Do you know what I mean?" she asked him. "Where are all the good guys? All the good girls, for that matter? And slapping me like that...at work!" She paused, waving an angry index finger at Reese and adding, "You know, I'd be justified in slapping her with an assault charge or two." Then she shook her head—felt her shoulders sagging defeatedly. "But then...would I be any better than her? And where would it get me? In debt to some attorney." Breck sighed heavily and rubbed at her temples for a moment. "What a rotten day," she muttered as she felt any remaining energy drain from her being.

"And it's only going to get worse, I'm afraid," Reese said, taking his keys from his worn-out jeans pocket, "'cause you do need a couple of stitches. Let's go."

Breck wiped the tears from her cheeks, but more still came as Reese nodded toward his office door.

"Come on," he said. "I'll take you to the Urgent Care down the road."

Breck shook her head. "You don't have to take me," she told him. After all, she didn't want to inconvenience him and add to his rotten day. "I can take myself."

"You'll be sitting there for at least two hours," he reminded her. "Urgent Care is just another term for Non-Urgent Care. But...it'll be faster than the emergency room." He grinned at her and opened his office door, gesturing for her to leave first. "You'll need something to do while you're waiting. You can talk to me."

Even with everything she'd gone through—the pain on her cheeks, the disappointment in humanity in her heart—she felt butterflies rise in her stomach, excited by the prospect of a couple of hours spent with Reese outside the office.

"Are you okay?" Patty asked as Breck reached under her desk to retrieve her purse.

"I'm fine," Breck lied.

"Patty…will you let Mr. Wilson know what's gone on, please? Will you tell him I'm running Breck down for stitches and that I'll get with him about this mess when I get back?" Reese asked.

"I sure will," Patty said, winking at Breck.

Breck was delighted when Reese then took hold of her arm and began walking with her out of the office. "Come on then, Miss McCall. Let's get you patched up."

Breck wiped a final tear from her cheek, knowing, however, that more would follow. It had been a terrible day, and even though she was in the company of her dreamy Reese Thatcher for now, she knew that anxiety would wash over her later.

"Climb on in," Reese said as he opened the door to just about the most beaten-up old blue pickup Breck had ever seen. Breck smiled at him as she stepped up into the passenger's side of the truck. Given his attire that day and his mode of transportation, he looked as if he could've just stepped out of her uncle's barn on the old McCall ranch.

As Reese shut her in and walked around the pickup to get in himself, Breck took a quick look around inside. Now this was a real man's truck, she noted. Gum wrappers littered the faded dashboard; there was a long crack in the windshield running vertically down in front of her. The gearshift was so old and so well used that the gear numbers were completely worn off. There was a distinct aroma in it as well—a combination of Speed Stick, mint gum, and soil. Not the expected vehicle choice of a man who made far beyond six figures annually.

"Buckle up," he said, grinning as he hopped into the truck and turned the ignition.

Breck smiled as she buckled the vintage seat belt, lap belt only, across her tummy and cinched it tight. She thought she might burst into beams of joy as he pulled the old cap from his back pocket, slapped it onto his head facing backward, and pulled a stick of gum from the pack lodged in the ashtray.

How cute! Breck thought as she watched him toss the empty wrapper onto the dashboard. He kept the gum in the old ashtray and threw the wrappers around everywhere.

"Gum?" he asked when he caught her staring at him with a smile.

"Sure," she said, taking a piece from the tray.

As she began folding the wrapper, intending to

put it in her purse, he said, "Just throw it up here." He tapped on the dashboard with one hand. "I'll get it later."

The local country music station playing on the radio and the way the old truck rode reminded Breck of her grandfather McCall's truck—heavy and tossing its passengers around like popcorn in a kettle.

Breck couldn't help smiling as she looked over at Reese, driving his old truck, chomping on his gum, and looking like a farm kid let loose in the city. He just kept getting better and better, and her heart felt heavy for a moment at knowing how slim her chances really were of winning him. Still, he had dressed up like her Highwayman. And he had kissed her pretty darn passionately. Breck studied him for a moment as he drummed on the steering wheel, matching the rhythm of the song currently playing on the radio.

"I know, I know," Reese said, smiling at her when he caught her staring at him. "Don't feel bad. Chicks always dig this pickup."

Breck giggled. "Chicks? Dig?" she teased.

"Yeah," he chuckled. "I think there's a song along those lines, isn't there?"

"Yeah," Breck agreed.

❦

Ten minutes later, Breck was sitting next to Reese, waiting her turn to be seen by an on-call doctor at the Urgent Care. Reese sat reading a pamphlet on hearing loss, and Breck looked around the waiting room trying to feign indifference to his presence.

"Yep," Reese said. "I'm a candidate."

"What?" Breck asked.

"A candidate. For hearing loss," he explained. "See? Use of loud machinery, listening to loud music, chronic ear infections as a child. It's a wonder I can still hear at all." Then he tossed the pamphlet to the chair next to him and began tapping his foot. "What do you want to do while we're waiting?" he asked.

"You don't really have to wait with me, Mr. Thatcher," Breck said, not wanting to inconvenience him any further. "I can call someone to—"

"How many times have you had stitches?" he interrupted.

Breck giggled. He was like a little boy trapped in a Sunday school meeting on an inviting summer's day.

"Never had any," she answered.

"What?" he exclaimed in sincere disbelief. "How can you never have had stitches before?"

"I don't know," she told him. "How many times have you had stitches?"

"Fifty-seven," he said.

"Fifty-seven?" Breck exclaimed. "How can you possibly have had to have stitches fifty-seven times?"

"The first time I slammed my finger in the door when I was two. Then there was the snowmobile accident I had when I was nineteen...drove my ride into a barbed-wire fence. Odds and ends and a couple of other big incidents. It's easy enough to need stitches," he told her. He talked so nonchalantly about it.

Breck shook her head, completely amused by his attitude.

"These won't hurt much though," he said, studying her cheek again. He took her chin in his hand and, frowning, looked at the wound more closely. "It ticks me off. I've been telling Mr. Wilson that Jamie was going to cause trouble. It makes me wonder what she has on him to make him keep her this long."

Breck nodded. "Me too," she admitted.

"Let her charge me with harassment," he growled. "I'll just insist she wears that shirt she wore today to court. Once the judge gets a load of that…I'll be fine."

Breck began to giggle—the sort of nervous giggle a person gets when a situation is too ridiculous, horrible, or both to believe. "That was the most outrageous blouse I've ever seen."

"Yes, ma'am," Reese chuckled. Breck glanced at him. There was something more real about Reese Thatcher that day. All the things that made him attractive were still there—surreal good looks, charming personality— but there was more. As Breck watched him sitting next to her, she sensed there was a part of him that had been hidden—or asleep—before. What was it?

"Do you have any brothers and sisters?" he asked, trying to make light conversation.

"One brother is all," Breck answered. "Jake. He's a Marine and stationed overseas."

"Really?" Reese seemed impressed. "Wow. Are you guys close?"

Breck shrugged. "As close as we can be now that he's so far away." She smiled at him. "You?"

"Two brothers, one older, one younger…and an older sister," he answered.

"That's great," Breck said, smiling. She liked imagining Reese as a child—playing and fighting with siblings.

"Mom and dad?" he asked.

"Yeah. They're in Europe for a few months."

Reese frowned. "So…you're alone here?"

"My uncles and cousins live a couple of hours away." Breck shrugged. She did miss her family. It broke Breck's heart the way families were separated by the necessity of earning a living or other intrusive elements of life. Modern times had wreaked havoc on the family unit. More often than not, Breck dreamed of living in the days when, in most cases, at least a few members of a person's family settled in close.

"Your mom and dad?" she asked, trying to change her lonely state of mind.

"One of each," Reese answered.

An awkward silence followed, and Breck understood why. Reese and she had shared only a working relationship, but the events that unfolded at Marcelli's a few nights before, coupled with today's goings-on, had given them a more intimate association—sort of.

"Why is it that you're not settled down…married and expecting a baby or two, Miss McCall?" His question was completely unanticipated and completely stunning.

"What?" was all Breck could muster.

Reese shook his head. "I don't know. You just seem...I mean, you're really good at what you do," he assured her. "It's just that...somehow I envision you in a little yellow house, surrounded by a white picket fence...a couple of babies crawling around while you bake chocolate-chip cookies or something."

Breck felt a crimson blush rise to her cheeks—accompanied by a delighted smile. It was as if he'd seen her soul! For in truth, that was exactly her secret, unspoken dream. Ever since she was a child she'd wanted to grow up, get married, and raise a family. But people, especially other women, seemed to frown on that way of life these days. And finding a man who wanted the same things seemed almost impossible. But here, sitting next to her in the Urgent Care...

"I'd love that!" she slipped. She hadn't meant to confess it to him so honestly. When he looked at her with curiosity, she continued, "It's just that...that's a vanishing way of life. Don't you think?"

He seemed thoughtful for a moment. "I guess so. But I think people allowed it to vanish. They get caught up in technology, entertainment. Or they run away from it for some reason." He looked at her again. "Had you pegged though. Didn't I?" He smiled.

Breck giggled. "That is what you do." After all, he wasn't a success in his field for no reason.

"That is what I do," he repeated. But as he looked at the

pretty girl sitting next to him in the Urgent Care, he couldn't help pushing the issue.

"Why don't you settle down, raise a family? Bake some cookies?" he asked. Reese knew he liked this girl way too much. He wasn't even sure she needed stitches. He'd just wanted to find a way to whisk her away from that awful office. She didn't belong there. He'd known it all along. He'd become far too protective of Breck McCall and her refreshing wholesomeness.

He smiled as she squirmed, uncomfortable by either his gaze or his question. He couldn't tell which.

"I…well…the opportunity hasn't presented itself," came her canned answer. Reese was in far too teasing a mood to let her slip away that easily.

"Which opportunity?" he asked. "To bake cookies or have babies?" He could've sworn she blushed to the very tips of her toes.

"T-to settle down," she stammered. "I bake cookies all the time."

"Breck McCall?" the nurse called from the front desk. Reese was disappointed that they'd called her in so quickly. He'd been hoping for at least two hours in her company.

❦

"Here," Reese said, taking Breck's keys. "Let me get it." Reese unlocked the door and stepped aside to allow Breck to enter her apartment first. Breck smiled, delighted with his manners. It had been a very long time since any man under the age of fifty had opened a door for her. And Reese had held doors for her all day.

Breck stepped into the apartment and somehow felt nervous as Reese stepped in after her, closing the door behind him. She watched as he began to look around.

Yep. Even the decor in her apartment—the atmosphere inside, the perfect feel of it—added to Reese's knowledge that this girl was different from most. First of all, it smelled like apples and cinnamon, nutmeg and warm bread—aromas he hadn't enjoyed for a long time.

"Would you like some ice water? Root beer?" Breck asked. He smiled, delighted with her concern for him and further delighted by what she had offered him to drink. Most women he'd known lately would've started with, *Can I get you a drink before I slip into something more comfortable?*

"Water," he answered, smiling at her. It seemed odd, but she looked adorable with her two little cheek stitches. He was mad for a moment again then—mad that a woman like Jamie even existed to harm such a sweet girl as this.

As Breck left the room to retrieve his water, Reese wandered around slowly—taking in everything about it. There was a small entertainment unit on a nearby wall, a TV, stereo, and DVD player housed there. Along the top stood an ancient-looking clock, nine or ten old sepia-toned photographs of people from days gone by. Reese looked closely at all the photographs for a moment. One in particular caught his interest—a handsome-looking couple standing with a horse. The woman was dark-haired and quite beautiful—especially for the time period, which Reese guessed was the late 1800s. In the background was an arched entry typical of an old ranch that read, "El Costa Lotta—McCall Ranch." Reese felt his eyebrows rise as he recognized the name of the ranch. McCall horses had been a valuable commodity in Colorado for the past century, and he figured that his own little Breck McCall must be a relative.

He looked down then—having nearly stepped on a pile of CDs and DVDs that lay on the floor in front of the wall unit. He smiled as he recognized artists and titles of bygone eras—old movie musicals from the '50s, jazz artists and crooners from the '40s, counted among various Christmas music and romantic comedies.

Looking around the room, he noted several antique lamp tables topped with hurricane lamps, old books on several wall bookshelves, three thriving Boston ferns. Artificial pumpkins and turkeys were strategically placed here and there, reflecting the woman's adoration of autumn and the holidays.

Indeed, it was a cozy, warm, beautiful room that left Reese in a fog of nostalgia, comfort, and further confirmation of Breck's being unique from other young women of the day.

"Here you go," she said, returning and handing him a glass of water.

"Thank you," he said. Even the water from her faucet tasted better. Purer, colder, fresher.

She bit her lip nervously and finally said, "Do you want to sit down for a moment?"

"Sure," Reese answered. He couldn't help grinning at her because he knew he made her uncomfortable. It probably wasn't easy to have her boss there in her apartment so unexpectedly. Especially when he'd kissed her just days before—and wanted to kiss her again—although she didn't know that. Even so, he enjoyed watching her discomfort.

"So," he began, sighing as he took a seat on her sofa, "this is where you live and bake cookies."

"Yep," was all she managed to say.

"And pumpkin pies that are better than my mother's," he added. She smiled, obviously delighted by his compliment. "It's nice," he told her. "I like it. It's very…you."

"What do you mean?" she asked, seeming uncertain as to whether this remark were a compliment.

"You know…comfortable, cozy…smells good," he answered. He smiled as he saw her cheeks go crimson.

"Thank you," she said. Then she dropped her gaze for a moment, her hands fiddling in her lap as she nearly mumbled, "Thank you…for taking me to get stitches."

"You're welcome," he said. "But a girl shouldn't have to leave an office job to go get sewn up."

"Maybe not," she said. "But thank you anyway."

He smiled, feeling a little angry with the male members of the human race. Obviously, she wasn't used to any sort of chivalry or manners in men. And he resented his own gender for that.

Breck tried to breathe regularly—tried not to smile too much at the joy she was experiencing. He was there—right there with her in her own apartment—Reese Thatcher! That fact was definitely worth getting beaten and having to have stitches. She couldn't believe he was there!

"I'll pick you up for work tomorrow, and you can just leave your car at the office tonight," he told her.

"Oh!" she exclaimed. She had forgotten all about her car. "Are you sure that will be all right? I can take the bus in and—" she began.

"No way," he said. "I'll just pick you up in the morning."

"If you're sure," she agreed.

"Of course I'm sure," he said. "I noticed the pictures on your thing there," he said, pointing to the wall unit. "Are you related to the people that run the McCall ranch out east of Colorado Springs?"

Breck felt her heart swell. He knew about the McCall ranch? How could he know? Of course, Reese Thatcher did seem to know something about everything.

"Yeah," Breck admitted with obvious pride. "My uncle runs it now...but my great-grandfather, Jackson McCall, named it officially back in, like, 1889."

"El Costa Lotta," Reese chuckled. "That's funny. I didn't get it at first."

"Yeah," Breck giggled. "Jackson McCall and his brothers were known as quite the characters in their day."

"You ever spend much time out there as a kid?" he asked.

Breck smiled, delighted by his interest. "I did," she told him. "And I loved it out there. I always wished my dad had stayed in the ranching business. But…he didn't."

Breck retrieved a drink coaster from the end table and handed it to Reese. He smiled at her and placed his glass on the coffee table in front of him.

Dang, this girl was cute! Reese felt a slight anxiety rising within him as he lingered in Breck's company. She was dangerous to a man's stability. He could feel it. A rare and wonderful girl like this could distract a guy from his course in life. He knew he had better escape while he could. Too much time around Breck McCall could be risky.

So, with a heavy sigh, Reese stood to leave. "I better get going," he told her. Her forced smile told him that she didn't want him to leave. No doubt the events of the day were still weighing heavily on her mind. Still, to linger would not be a good idea. She was too cute and vulnerable with her little stitches and windblown hair.

"Thank you for everything, Mr. Thatcher," she told him. And then he knew he had lingered too long. For the devil in him was at the door.

"You mean for taking you to the Urgent Care?" he said, smiling at her as she stood to face him. "Or do you mean for dressing up like an idiot for your birthday?"

She smiled and blushed. "Both," she said.

He watched her glance away shyly when he took her hand in his and said, "I'm sorry about this mess today, Breck."

"It wasn't your fault," she assured him.

"It was. I know that," he said. "You stuck up for me and ended up with stitches." She shook her head and glanced down shyly again. "And the worst part of it is...she was right."

She looked up at him—frowning—puzzled. "What do you mean?"

Stop it right now, Reese, he told himself. But it was too late. The wolf in him was already prowling. He raised her hand to his lips and placed a lingering kiss on the back of it.

"Only...it wasn't her that I planned on harassing." He grinned, delighted at the way her eyes widened in astonishment at his inference. She was struck silent, of course, so the wolf continued to stalk its prey. "Still... does it count as harassment if it's after hours and not in the office?"

"What?" she gulped.

Somewhere Reese found his steady mark then, and instead of stealing a kiss as he'd planned, he simply asked, "Can I take you to dinner Friday?"

"What?" she repeated, obviously still rattled by his previous flirtations.

"To help soothe the sting of what happened today...let me take you to dinner, Breck." She paused, seeming uncertain, so he added, "I'd feel a little better if you let me make a sad attempt at repaying you for looking out for me today."

She smiled at him. "Sure," she agreed.

Reese smiled at her. He seemed genuinely pleased that she'd accepted his dinner invitation. Breck tried to remain calm—tried to still her excited trembling until she'd seen him all the way out the door and closed it.

"Seven okay?" he asked.

"Seven what?" she asked in return. Kisses? Sure! She'd take seven kisses from him any day!

He chuckled. "Seven o'clock at night on Friday. I'll pick you up at seven. Okay?"

"Oh, yeah," Breck breathed, blushing and horrified from being so brainless for a moment.

"Okay," he said. "Call me if you need anything tonight."

"Thank you," Breck managed.

Through her front window she watched him walk out to his pickup. He smiled and waved to her a moment before he drove off into the sunset.

Breck sighed, content and delighted with the result of what had otherwise been a completely rotten day. Gently she touched the stitches that held the wound at her cheek. Yep! Well worth the pain to spend an afternoon with Reese Thatcher. How would she ever settle down, stay calm, and function normally until Friday night?

CHAPTER SIX

Tuesday, Wednesday, and Thursday seemed to drag by like months as Breck waited for Friday to arrive. Work seemed tedious at best, and working with Reese was all the more difficult now—for now she sensed she knew a part of him that had been dormant or hiding before. When she considered his willingness to play the Highwayman—thought of the way he had been dressed the day she'd been assaulted by Jamie Reynolds—even the type of vehicle he drove hinted at a hidden identity of some sort. For the most part, Reese perfectly fit the description of the up-and-coming, big-city businessman, but there was more to him than mere appearances. Breck was certain of it.

From the time Reese dropped her off at her apartment Monday afternoon until the moment the clock on her wall unit chimed seven on Friday night, Breck was preoccupied with anticipating the evening. How should she dress? He hadn't specified, nor had she thought to ask, what type of restaurant he was taking her to. So as she took a deep breath and readied to open the door to meet Reese, she smoothed the white angora sweater she'd chosen to wear with a jean skirt.

"Hi," Reese greeted her as she opened the door. He wore Levi's and a black long-sleeved shirt—perfect as usual and handsome as a dream!

"Hi," she replied.

"You ready?" he asked.

She nodded, taking her coat from the peg behind the door. Breck locked her apartment door and then began walking toward the street, where she could see Reese's pickup parked.

"You look great," he said, smiling at her and placing a hand at the small of her back. Breck felt herself blush and hoped he would think it was just the cool night air.

Opening the passenger door first, Breck was startled when Reese simply spun her around to face him, placed his powerful hands at her waist, and lifted her into the pickup seat.

"Don't want you to tear your skirt," he explained before closing the door.

"Thank you," Breck offered, blushing with the delight borne of his rather heroic gesture.

"I hope you like steak," Reese told her as his pickup's engine roared to life, "and company."

Breck felt her heart sink to the pit of her stomach. He'd invited someone else?

"Sure," she said, forcing a smile and trying to sound delighted.

"Good. 'Cause we're going to Bulls Eye's, and my mom is meeting us there," he explained. Breck glanced at him, her mouth gaping open in astonishment. Oh, it wasn't the fact that he was taking her to the most expensive steak house in the city that shocked her: it was the fact that his mother was meeting them there! His mother?

"Your mother?" she couldn't help asking.

"Yeah," he said, smiling. "She ran up to check on me today and decided to stay the night. I told her I had a date...but how could I leave her alone? You know?"

Breck shivered with excitement at his referring to their dinner as a date. Still, his mother?

"Of course you couldn't," she said. "I wouldn't expect you to."

"Oh, I would've just given her a book or the remote or something, and she would've been glad to stay home. But..." he continued, "she found out I was going with you. That's why she wanted to come."

Breck felt nauseated. "Why would it matter that it was me?" she ventured.

"Really?" he chuckled. "Are you kidding? You're the pumpkin sweater girl. I suspect she wants to see what kind of a girl would get me to go the extra mile for a birthday gift."

"Oh. I see." Breck swallowed hard. All at once her excitement about the evening had disappeared. His mother, for Pete's sake!

The rest of the way to the restaurant they talked about nothing in particular—the Broncos' last game, the Allen case, other things in the news. Breck thought her knees would fail her when, at last, they did arrive and Reese took her hand to help her down out of the pickup. He did not release her hand as he locked up the truck and started into the restaurant either. Her hand burned warm and tingly when he held it, and even when they entered Bulls Eye's to be greeted by Reese's mother, he did not let her hand go.

"Hey, Mom," Reese said, kissing his mother affectionately on one cheek. "This is Breck. The pumpkin sweater girl."

Reese's mother was a short, plump, merry-looking woman. Her eyes seemed to smile along with the rest of her face, which was framed by brown hair with just a hint of gray. She wore a bright red sweater under a denim jacket, a jean skirt, and a pair of red Ropers. She was absolutely the friendliest, most approachable-looking woman Breck had ever met.

"Oh, hello!" Reese's mother greeted, throwing her arms around Breck's shoulders in a familiar hug. "I'm so glad to meet you…Breck, is it?"

"Yes, ma'am," Breck said, smiling. "And it's so nice to meet you, Mrs. Thatcher."

"Oh, call me Marjie," she said, laughing.

"And I'd like to thank you for the beautiful sweater. I've never seen anything like it! It's so perfect," Breck said.

"You're welcome. Aren't you a sweetheart?" Marjie cooed, delighted by the praise.

As the waitress led them to their table, Marjie said, "I hope you don't mind my comin' along on your date tonight, Breck."

"Oh, of course not," Breck told her. And, surprisingly, she realized she meant it.

"I just swung up to town to check on Reese and do some shoppin' today...didn't think that he might have plans." Breck watched as the small woman squiggled into her chair at their table. It was like some sort of strange white light radiated from her. Breck would have sworn that she illuminated the room all on her own.

"Now, don't eat like a bird, Mom," Reese said as the waitress handed them all menus. "I mean for you to go home well-fed and rested."

"And I mean to go home that way," Marjie said, opening her menu and happily sighing.

Breck was feeling quite comfortable considering the circumstances. The more she thought about it, the more she realized how sweet it was that Reese was taking his mother to dinner with them.

"Reese tells me you're related to the McCalls out at El Costa Lotta," Marjie said as she flipped a page on her menu.

"Oh, yes. Jackson McCall was my great-grandfather," Breck explained.

"Good horses comin' out of there these past couple of years," Marjie said, nodding. "Ol' Goose was from the McCall place, Reese," she added.

"He was a good horse for kids," Reese said.

And then, it all became clear to Breck. How could she have been so naive? So blind?

"You're a farm boy!" she exclaimed, looking to Reese in astonishment. She could see it now—the polite manners, the sauntering way of walking, the pickup, the knowledge of the McCall ranch. Instantly, she felt like a cloud had been lifted from her mind.

Reese and his mother both chuckled. "It's been a long time since anyone called me a boy, Breck," he told her.

Breck giggled. "It just explains so much." Immediately she wished she wouldn't have said anything at all.

For Reese instantly asked, "Like what?" His tone seemed a little defensive, and when his mother reached over and patted his arm, Breck feared she might have offended him.

"Well…like your good manners, your old pickup… things like that," she stammered.

He sighed and smiled at her. "It shows, huh?"

"It better show!" Marjie said. "I worked hard raisin' you into a gentleman."

Breck couldn't quit smiling at Reese. It was like the last piece to the puzzle—the puzzle that was the man Reese Thatcher—had just been pressed into place. All this time Breck had tried to put her finger on just what was different about Reese other than heavenly good looks, success, strength—other than the obvious. Now she knew—and she loved him all the more for it! Yes, loved him, she admitted to herself.

The meal was delicious, the conversation happy and light, and Breck began to dread its end. She concluded that Marjie Thatcher was an angel—a hard-working, old-fashioned girl who loved her family. Reese seemed to relax in his mother's presence to a state that Breck had certainly never witnessed, and it was wonderful—like sitting before a warm, cozy fire on a cold winter's night.

Breck was just finishing her last bite of chocolate cake when Marjie asked, "So, Breck…what are your plans for Thanksgivin'?"

Truly taken by surprise and not foreseeing what was about to come next, Breck stammered, "Oh, I… uh…" For in truth, she had no plans. With her parents in Europe and brother, Jake, overseas, she had simply reconciled herself to sitting at home with a turkey potpie.

"So you don't have plans?" Marjie prodded.

"Well, not really. My parents are in Europe this year, and my brother is in the military, so I thought I might just—"

"Reese!" Marjie interrupted, turning to her son. "You have to bring her out to the farm for Thanksgivin'!"

"Oh! No, no, no," Breck assured her. "I have a ton of people that I can—"

"No. I won't hear of it. You've got to come with Reese out to the farm and have Thanksgivin' with us," Marjie insisted. "Besides, if Reese is given the responsibility of bringin' our guest…then he won't be able to find an excuse not to come."

"Mom," Reese scolded, "don't force her to come if she doesn't want to." He was shaking his head and smiling—amused at his mother's insistent manner.

"She wants to come. Don't you, Breck?" Marjie said.

This was uncharted territory for Breck. An invitation to Thanksgiving? From her boss's mother? What was she supposed to do?

"I couldn't possibly impose like that, Mrs. Thatcher. It just isn't done and—" Breck began to argue.

"Impose? Are you kiddin'? We would love to have you! You'll come out for the whole four days, won't you?" Marjie continued, "Reese, you are givin' her those days off, aren't you?"

"Four days?" Breck exclaimed.

"Yes, Mom…she has the whole time off," Reese chuckled. "But maybe she doesn't want to come."

"You do want to come, don't you?" Marjie pleaded.

"I-I can't possibly…" But the refusal stuck in Breck's throat like a horsefly, for the look on Mrs. Thatcher's face was so sincere—so pleading—and she knew refusal would hurt her. Reese's also wore an expression that said she should not deny his mother. A kind of *please don't hurt my mother's feelings* sort of expression.

"Of course you can!" Marjie announced, finally. "You can drive up on Wednesday night with Reese. Can't she, Reese?"

"Of course," Reese said, smiling at Breck. She knew he could sense her squirming under the pressure of the situation.

"Just pack up a few things and spend the weekend with us! I promise it will be worth your time," Marjie assured her.

"But, Mrs. Thatcher...I just couldn't. It would be..." Breck stumbled over her words like they were choking her. For one thing, she couldn't imagine anything more wonderful than spending four days in the company of Reese Thatcher. Add to it the fact that just being out of the city would be the stuff of dreams—but she couldn't possibly accept. Could she?

"I won't take no for an answer," Marjie said, smiling. "And, furthermore, I won't go home here in a few minutes so that Reese can take you out parking, if you don't agree."

Again Breck's mouth gaped open in astonishment—her face as red as Marjie Thatcher's sweater.

"Mom," Reese scolded, "quit trying to bully her into it." Then, smiling, he turned to Breck and said, "Come on, Breck. Just agree to it so we can go somewhere and park."

Breck could only sit, silent. Was he kidding? Was his mother kidding? But when they both looked at her—eyes smiling with mischief—she knew they had only been teasing her.

"Oh, please say yes, Breck," Marjie pleaded at last. "It will be a Thanksgivin' you'll never forget. I promise."

Breck looked into the woman's twinkling eyes. How could she refuse to go?

"Okay...I guess it would be all right," she managed.

Reese's mother clapped her hands together, delighted. "Wonderful!" she exclaimed. "Now, Reese... I'll just be on my way," she began, standing as if she were leaving. "I've got my key to the house, and I'll just put my little self sound to sleep in your guest room for the night. You and Breck finish up your evenin'."

"You're leaving?" Breck asked.

Marjie smiled, hugged Breck, kissed Reese on the cheek, and said, "Of course. I've spoiled your evenin' enough already."

As quick as that, she was gone. She was gone, and Breck sat stunned—unbelieving she'd been talked into going to her boss's parents' house for Thanksgiving.

"Don't worry, Breck," Reese said, motioning to the waiter to bring him the bill. "It'll be fun." Still she couldn't speak. Reese chuckled. "What's the matter?"

"I'm just wondering..." Breck began, "how I got here."

Reese put a hundred dollar bill on the table with the tab, stood, and pulled Breck's chair out for her. "That's my mother for you," he sighed. "When she likes somebody...she doesn't hide it. She'll be gushing on about you for days now."

"But I didn't do anything," Breck reminded him.

"That's the point," he said. "You were just you."

Breck noticed the way the women in the restaurant followed Reese's every movement as they walked between tables and past booths on their way out. She couldn't help the feeling of pride that swelled in her at being on the arm of such a man. On top of everything else, he treated his mother like a queen. Breck decided not to let discouragement or uncertainty overtake her. For the moment, she would just bask in his presence— bathe in everyone else's envy.

"How are your stitches healing?" Reese asked as the pickup hummed along the interstate.

"Fine," Breck said. "The redness is gone, and it doesn't hurt nearly as much now."

"It left a nice bruise though," he noted. And it was true. Breck had tried to forget about it. But, yes, her cheek was a lovely color of mingled purples, yellows, and greens. "It still ticks me off."

"At least she's not around the office anymore," Breck said. "It was worth getting a shiner just for that to happen."

Reese's silence implied that he wasn't sure he agreed with her. Therefore, she let the subject die.

"I'm planning on leaving the Wednesday morning before Thanksgiving," he suddenly told her. "I'll okay the day off for you too."

Looking to him, she said, "I just don't think I can—"

"Oh, there's no squirming out of it now, baby," he chuckled. Breck was a bit caught off guard by his rather endearing term. "Mom will have me skinned alive if I don't bring you now."

He'd called her baby, and she'd loved the way he said it—so naturally—as if he truly meant it!

"You better bring some warm clothes. There's already snow out at the place," he said. "And I'll tell Mom you'll bring some pumpkin pies."

"Oh, no!" Breck argued. If there was one thing she knew, it was that a woman needed to feel like she was the queen of her own castle. "Can't I bring something else?"

"No way!" Reese said, with the lack of understanding akin to a man. "Mom *has* to taste your pie."

Reese parked the pickup in front of Breck's apartment building, and she felt the cold rain of disappointment begin to envelop her. Her night with Reese was over.

He got out of the pickup, opened Breck's door, helped her out, and began walking with her toward her apartment. When they reached the apartment door, Breck pulled her keys from her purse and began to fiddle with them.

"Here," Reese said, taking the keys from her. He opened her door and let her step inside.

"Thank you for dinner," Breck said, feeling suddenly very shy—like a high school girl returning from her first prom.

Reese leaned in the door toward her. "You're not mad at me, are you?" he asked.

"Whatever for?" Breck asked, her attention falling to his mouth.

He grinned and said, "For bringing my mom to dinner with us."

Breck shook her head and smiled at him. "No. She's adorable. And it was so fun to watch the two of you together."

"Yeah, but now you're all committed to Thanksgiving. Heck, I'm all committed to Thanksgiving," he said.

Breck thought it odd that he should refer to himself

as being committed to be with his family on the one holiday that most families tried to be together.

"Don't you usually go home for Thanksgiving?" she couldn't help asking.

Reese sighed. "That's a long story, Breck." She knew this was a sensitive subject, something he wasn't ready to reveal to her. Nor should she expect him to. Then looking at her, his eyes narrowing, a mischievous grin spreading across his face, he said, "That's a soft-looking sweater you're wearing."

"Thank you," she said, uncertain where he was going with this compliment.

But as he stepped through the door and reached out, taking her by the waist with one hand and brushing her sore cheek with the other, she began to hope—to hope and to tremble.

"And your poor little stitches," he mumbled as he seemed to look intently at her cheek for a moment. "You know," he continued, "it would make me feel a lot better about what happened on Monday if you kissed me good night."

"It would?" she whispered, awed by his suggestion.

"Oh yeah," he assured her, his grin broadening to a smile.

"But you're my boss," Breck reminded him.

"So?" he chuckled. "It isn't like we haven't done it before."

Breck felt his arms around her then, pulling her against his strong body. She looked up at him, her mouth moist with the desire for him to follow through with his implication—to kiss her.

"Hmm. This *is* a soft sweater," he whispered a moment before she felt him playfully kiss her upper lip. She gasped quietly, as he then kissed her lower lip twice in succession before finally pressing his mouth to hers in a tender, yet powerful exchange. Breck felt an overwhelming heat travel up the length of her spine, spreading throughout her limbs. The feel of Reese's roughly shaven face against the flesh of her face as he kissed her served to somehow further elevate her temperature, and she worried that she might melt dead away in his arms.

His kiss became driven—impassioned for a moment—then he simply pulled away from her, sighed heavily, and said, "And now...I better be going." Smiling at her, he added, "I guarantee you my mom did not go to bed when she got back to my place. She's waiting up to make sure I didn't let you squiggle out of coming for Thanksgiving."

Breck was speechless. All she could do was smile and nod at him. He turned and began walking down the sidewalk to his pickup.

As Breck watched him, he turned to look at her and said, "I'm beginning to like Friday nights, Miss McCall."

Breck smiled and waved as he drove away. What was happening? Could it be that she'd actually managed to capture Reese Thatcher's attention? Or had she simply captured his mother's attention somehow? All mothers wanted their sons to have nice girls in their lives. Still, Reese had kissed her again—and it was rapturous! She dared to hope then—dared to hope that Thanksgiving would be special. She just hoped she'd be able to find the courage to follow through with it. The girls would help her with that. Yes—the girls would help her find the strength.

That night Breck lay awake for hours unable to settle her mind or her senses, which had both been so completely stirred up by Reese Thatcher that evening. Thanksgiving was all she could think about. Four days with Reese, away from the city, away from work. Could another warm, delicious kiss with him be in her future? But what then? She wouldn't worry about what then. She'd simply worry about Thanksgiving.

Gazing at the picture of her and Reese kissing—the photograph of her and her Highwayman hanging on her bedroom wall—Breck tried to believe that there was still hope in the world—that people could stay faithful in marriage, that nasty troublemakers like Jamie Reynolds did not make up the majority of the population. Maybe dreams could come true. Maybe.

Just as Reese suspected, his mother was sitting on the sofa, eyes beaming with curiosity when he arrived home after dropping Breck off at her apartment. He chuckled, for he could see that Marjorie Thatcher was near to exploding from the pressure of so many withheld questions.

"Well?" she asked.

"Well what?" He'd toy with her a bit. It always amused him how wound up his mother got about certain things—like Christmas, new puppies, and the possibility of romance in the lives of her children.

"Oh, don't play dumb with me, Reese Thatcher!" she scolded. "What's goin' on with you and that lovely girl?"

Reese shrugged. "What do you mean, Mom? She had a bad day at work on Monday. She's my assistant… thought I'd take her to dinner to—"

"She's your assistant who had a bad day, my hind end." Marjie wagged an index finger at her son. "You didn't flinch once when I invited her for Thanksgiving. Day was you would've walked in here ranting and raving like a madman had I done that." Again Reese shrugged. His mother continued, "And I don't ever recall you havin' me knit anything for a girl before."

"Calm down, Mom," Reese told her, still smiling. "You're getting all worked up over nothing."

Marjie sighed, defeated. Waving an arm in the air as she turned toward the guest room, she said, "Oh, you just go on ahead and act like I can't read you like a book, boy. 'Cause I can. And that girl is on your mind."

"Good night, Mom," he called after her. It was true. She could read him like a book—always had. But he wasn't ready to tell her anything about Breck. He was still too unsettled himself. And the truth was Breck was getting deeper and deeper under his skin.

He shouldn't have kissed her just now. He was her boss! But he couldn't resist her—there in that soft, furry sweater, those two little pitiful stitches on her tender, bruised cheek. Besides, he'd waited a week to kiss her again. And considering the feelings that had been rolling around in him since that night at Marcelli's, he figured he'd done a pretty good job at keeping his hands off.

However, four days down at his parents' farm? Temptation would be thicker than the November fog. And Reese Thatcher knew one thing—he'd lost himself years ago, and until he was found, he'd have to avoid dragging anyone else down with him.

As he lay in bed late that night staring out the window at the stars, he knew there was something very different about Breck McCall. For one thing, she kept distracting him from all the down and dirty cases he was working on at the office. She was like a sweet beacon of sunshine beckoning at the mouth of a dark cave of worldly sludge.

With a heavy sigh, Reese rolled over, punched his pillow a couple of times, and mumbled, "Guess I'm going home for Thanksgiving this year." He caught himself smiling at the thought.

CHAPTER SEVEN

"This is it!" Sherryl squealed, leaping up from Breck's sofa like a recently released jack-in-the-box. "Home to meet the family? Oh, this is big!"

"You guys," Breck began. From the moment her friends had shown up for a night of silliness at Breck's apartment—from the moment two weeks ago when she'd told them all about her dinner with Reese and his mother, her invitation for Thanksgiving—not one of them had retained a calm thread of sanity. "She was just being nice," Breck continued.

"A woman doesn't invite just anybody to Thanksgiving dinner—hold on, Thanksgiving weekend—hold on, the entire four-day break. A woman just doesn't invite anybody...and certainly not just to be nice, Breck," Trixie interjected.

"That's right," Barb agreed. "My mother-in-law still doesn't invite me." Everyone giggled.

"And you'll have to bring something as a token of your thanks," Kay mused, frowning.

"I've got it!" Sherryl exclaimed. "I'll make an

enlargement of that picture of you and Reese making out at Marcelli's!"

"Funny, Sherr," Breck giggled. "Very funny." Her friends were absolutely no help, and that's why she loved them. Oh, they had plenty of serious talks together—heartfelt sobbing over trial and tribulations. But moments like these—moments when all care was thrown to the wind, discouragement vanquished in favor of glee and fun—those were the moments that pulled Breck through. Those were the moments she most looked forward to.

"But, Breck," Kay began, clasping one of Breck's hands in her own. "Don't you feel it? Something big is about to happen."

Breck inhaled a deep breath, trying to calm her nerves. She did feel it. But was it a premonition of good—or an ominous throbbing of impending disappointment?

"You should definitely take your pumpkin flannels," Trixie suggested.

"Heck, no!" Barb argued. "You need something more alluring…like that flannel nightgown with the little pink sheep on it."

"Absolutely not!" Sherryl exclaimed. "She'll look like a pilgrim."

"Well, it will be Thanksgiving weekend," Kay pointed out.

"Guys…no one will be seeing my pajamas while I'm there," Breck said. Her friends exchanged skeptical glances.

"Ten to one…they're the kind of family where the mom makes everyone matching pajama bottoms for Christmas," Barb said. "They probably eat breakfast in them."

"They're farmers, Barb," Breck pointed out. "They probably do two hours of chores before breakfast."

"Still, you can never go on the assumption that you won't be seen in your nightwear," Kay instructed.

"What about those plaid ones she has?" Trixie asked. "They're kind of silky and pretty."

Breck giggled and covered her face with her hands for a moment. These friends of hers were unbelievable! Here she was, on the verge of the most nerve-wracking weekend of her life, and all they could discuss was what she should wear to sleep in. Oh, how she loved them for it!

Oddly enough, the weeks since Reese's mother had invited Breck to visit for Thanksgiving had passed fairly quickly. Work had gone smoothly—save the fact that Jamie Reynolds had attempted a lawsuit against Wilson Investigation. That had been quickly vanquished, however—the moment Jamie's attorney had seen the security camera footage of her slapping Breck. Even the Allen case had simmered down for the moment. Still, there were plenty of ugly cases hitting Breck's desk. Reese had been gone for a few days, and Breck found it much easier to work with him out of the office. He was more distracting to her than ever. Fortunately, the girls—Trixie, Barb, Sherryl, and Kay—had helped

Breck to remain calm, to look to a positive outcome concerning her trip to Reese's home.

And now, unbelievably, here she sat, in Reese's pickup—on her way to his family's farm for Thanksgiving.

"I can't believe I'm doing this," Breck mumbled as they hit the interstate and headed south. All at once her nerves twisted themselves into knots, and she worried she might be ill. "I think you better take me back. I'm not sure I can go through with this," she told him.

Reese smiled, "You're not going skydiving, Breck," he told her. "You're just going to the Thatcher's farm for Thanksgiving."

For a moment, Breck considered how much easier skydiving seemed. Rather a few minutes of terror than an entire weekend of it.

"But this is so out of my comfort zone," Breck explained.

Reese chuckled. "It's a little out of mine too…if it makes you feel any better," he said.

"What do you mean?" she asked. He was going home for Thanksgiving. She assumed he would be excited—view it as a holiday routine. Hadn't he always gone home for Thanksgiving?

"I haven't gone home for Thanksgiving for the past two years," he confessed.

"What?" Breck was stunned. "Why not?" Immediately she realized she probably shouldn't have asked the question. Most likely Reese's reasons for not going back were personal.

But he shrugged broad shoulders and said, "I always came up with a good excuse. At least, I thought they were good excuses."

"Why wouldn't you want to go?" Breck pressed. She was too deeply interested now to worry about being considerate.

"Honestly?" he asked. She nodded. "I think I didn't want to be reminded how great it was."

Breck was puzzled. "Why not?"

"Oh, it's a long story," he sighed. "And it's…it's…"

"Personal?" she finished. A girl! That was what it had to be. He'd had a girlfriend, and she'd broken his heart. Breck was immediately jealous of whoever the mystery girl was. She loathed her instantly.

"No, not really," he said. "Just stupid."

"Will you tell me?" she asked. She couldn't believe how bold she was being. But this had happened to her before. Every time she went out to El Costa Lotta to visit her cousins, in fact. Once she'd left the city, the pollution, the crowds—it was as if her soul could breathe again. She always felt free to be herself—more confident in who she was when she was away from the city.

Reese grinned and looked at her. "Are you serious?"

"Of course," she confirmed. "I can't imagine why a farm boy would rather stay in that smelly old city for Thanksgiving instead of escaping back home to family and good cooking."

Again he smiled. "You're certainly chatty this morning."

Breck shrugged. "Well, we do have...what? Two hours to kill. You might as well tell me your deepest, darkest secrets." She smiled at him, and he shook his head, amused.

"Well, if you insist on being bored to tears," he began, "I'll confess it all to you."

Breck smiled, snuggled down into her coat, and anxiously waited for him to begin.

"Okay, I'm ready," she said.

He chuckled, shook his head again, and turned the heater up a notch. "Okay, Miss McCall. But it's not a happy story."

A bit of Breck's enthusiasm was lost—but she was still far more than very interested.

"Well," he began, releasing a heavy sigh, "as you know, the grass is always greener."

"I know," she said, understanding the cliché. Things often looked better, more exciting, when you looked into the neighbor's yard.

"When you're young you think you know everything and associate all your troubles with the place you're at. You know?"

Breck nodded.

"Well, when I was about nineteen," he continued, "me and my friend Tom Holms were out on the snowmobiles. Just having a regular day of fun in the snow." Reese checked his rearview mirror, and Breck looked at him, waiting for him to go on with his story. "I'd had an accident earlier in the month...ran my ride right through a barbed-wire fence, and Mom had nearly grounded me from the snowmobiles for life," he continued.

"One of your fifty-seven sets of stitches?" Breck prodded.

Reese smiled, "Yeah. A big set." He continued then, "But Tom and I were daredevils. You know how boys that age are." Breck nodded. "Well, we were out by Simpson's Woods, a few miles east of our old farmhouse...and all of a sudden, I hear a rifle go off." Breck felt the hair on the back of her neck begin to prickle. She sensed this wasn't going to be one of the more lighthearted farm boy stories that Reese probably owned.

"It's not that unusual to hear gunfire out there... especially during elk season. But I stopped to check on Tom anyway, and when I turned around...his ride was stalled, and he was lying facedown in the snow." He paused, and his eyes narrowed with the unpleasant memory. "By the time I stopped and got to him, the snow around him was already red with his blood, and...he was dead."

Breck's mouth gaped open in surprise. She certainly hadn't expected such a revelation. She'd expected him to say he had become bored with farm life, had his heart broken by some girl, or something. Nothing like this.

"Reese!" Breck exclaimed in a whisper as she looked up at him.

"Nobody ever found out where the shot came from. It was elk season, after all, and people in town speculated that someone was out hunting, and Tom was hit by a stray shot. Or maybe some kids were messing around with guns somewhere. Either way, the sheriff's department never did figure it all out."

"I'm...I'm so sorry, Reese," Breck stammered. How did someone respond to such a story other than with an awkward apology?

Reese shrugged. "I left home that next year... earned a bachelor's in three years...then flushed it down the toilet and joined the Denver PD."

"A policeman?" Breck nearly gasped.

Reese smiled at her. "How do you think I got on at Wilson?" he asked. "Yep...went off to become a cop to make sure that every case in the entire world didn't remain unsolved like Tom's."

Breck felt her insides begin to tremble. The thought of Reese as a policeman unnerved her somehow. "But you quit," she offered.

"Yeah. Mom convinced me to. She said she could see how dealing with the scum of the earth was bringing me down. Plus, she worried a lot," he continued. "Farmers die of old age, heart attacks, or getting kicked in the head by a horse. The idea of me getting shot by a drug dealer was really causing her a lot of stress... depression. So when Mr. Wilson heard about me— that I was a good detective and how fast I had made it up the ladder—he offered me a job, and I took it." He paused. "Still trying to save the world...but with a little less danger to my person. Easier on my mother's nerves."

"Officer Thatcher?" Breck said, still stunned at Reese's revelation.

"Yeah," he chuckled. "Hard to imagine?"

"Well...sort of. Yes," Breck admitted.

"It wasn't for me. Mom knew that," he said. "It would've killed me one way or the other...physically or mentally."

Breck shivered at his statement—completely undone by the thought of Officer Thatcher being killed in the line of duty.

"And so...there you have it, Breck McCall," he sighed. "I got to where I just didn't go home very often because...I felt weak when I did."

"Weak?" Breck didn't understand. How could going home have made him feel weak? Strong families usually drew strength from one another.

"Yeah," he said. "Every time I go home, it gets harder and harder to leave. And I have to."

"Why?" she plainly asked. She knew she certainly wouldn't have left if she'd grown up at El Costa Lotta.

He smiled at her. "Boys are different than girls, Breck," he explained. "Initially I was angry...angry about Tom being killed and no one being able to tell me why. Then I took it upon myself to save the world from unsolved crime. Turned around and I was old enough I needed to make a living somehow, and I'd fallen into a great job that let me do both." He reached over and turned the heater down a notch. "But recently...recently I've been wondering if I really want to do what I'm doing."

Breck began to panic. Was he thinking of leaving Wilson? He couldn't! She would die without him there!

"So there you have it," he said, interrupting her thoughts. "My deep, dark secret."

"Wow," she breathed. "That's kind of hard for me to top."

He chuckled. "But you have to try. I told you one of mine. What's yours?"

But she couldn't possibly tell him. Her deepest, darkest secret was she was falling hopelessly in love with him! More and more every day. That she could not reveal.

"I don't think I have one that can measure up," she said.

"Hey. Fair is fair. You gotta spill something," he told her.

Breck searched the files of her memory for something, some secret she could share. But still the only one she could think of was she was in love with her boss.

"Come on now, Miss McCall," he chuckled. "Pay up."

But try as she might, she couldn't think of one thing, one delicious secret to share with him. "Can I have a few minutes?" she begged.

Reese playfully glared at her. "Okay. I'll let you off the hook. But just this once."

"My life just isn't as…as…involved as yours," she explained.

"Sure," he said.

Just then something clanked in the pickup bed as they hit a bump in the road.

"Did you pack those pies safe enough?" Reese asked, sincerely concerned. Breck smiled, amused by his infatuation with the four pumpkin pies he'd talked her in to bringing.

"Yes. They'll be fine," she assured him.

The knot of nerves began to form in her stomach again. What was she doing? She couldn't be going home with her boss for Thanksgiving. It was too…

"So let me tell you about the Thatcher family so that you'll be prepared. Okay?" Reese began. He was so talkative—and Breck liked it.

"Okay," she said.

"Mom you've met," he began, and Breck nodded. "And with Mom, or 'Marjie,' as she'll have you call her for now…what you see is what you get." He smiled. "Dad is hilarious. You'll like him. His name is Ben, and he's a typical farmer…hard-working, good sense of humor, and worn out by the end of the day." Breck smiled, knowing she would like Reese's dad for being a typical farmer. "My older sister, Katie, is married to Keith Donaldson, and they have a little girl who's, like, about four, I think…and another one who's, like, two." Reese paused, pensive for a moment. "Yeah. Four and two. Their names are Lizzy and Sarah. Then there's Bobby. He's just under Katie and not married yet… still living with Mom and Dad. I'm next, and my little brother, Nick, is the youngest. He's twenty by now. He lives with Mom and Dad too." He smiled at her. "And there you go," he said.

"Sounds quite intimidating," Breck sighed.

"There's nothing to worry about. You'll love my family," Reese assured her. And Breck had no doubt about it. "And they don't know anything about your weird friends or how they talked me into being a piece of beefcake for your birthday, or anything like that."

"What?" Breck exclaimed, blushing vermilion.

Reese laughed and then said, "Come on, Breck. You gotta admit, those girlfriends of yours go to some extreme measures." Breck could only nod in agreement. He was right, after all, and many were the times she'd been on the planning end of the measures. "All I have to say is you're one heck of a good sport."

"No," she corrected. "You're one heck of a good sport."

He nodded. "Yes, I am. But…I wasn't entirely the innocent participant you may think I was."

"What do you mean?" she asked.

"You seem to have forgotten that I placed a condition of my own on the event."

Breck thought back, but all she could remember now was how fabulous he'd looked in the costume of the Highwayman—how thirst-quenching his kiss had been.

"They paid you?" she thought out loud. She was horrified at considering it.

But before she could totally crush, he answered, "No. I told them I better get a kiss from you out of the deal. I made them swear to me you'd kiss me before I agreed to do it." Breck's mouth was gaping open again, and he laughed as he glanced at her. "I guess I'm just spilling secrets left and right."

He was right! She remembered now. *We promised him you'd kiss him too, Breck*, Barb had said that night. But amid all the excitement and passionate kissing, Breck had completely forgotten.

"You were a little freaked out, making it a little short-lived," he chuckled. "But it was nice. Wasn't it?" He was smiling at her, knowing full well how embarrassed she was.

She was mortified! She was elated! She was horrifyingly delighted! He'd wanted to kiss her. That's what it all boiled down to. He'd wanted to kiss her!

"You're redder than a beet in a basket," he laughed. "And with that, I'll let you off the hook for a minute or two." He chuckled some more and tuned the radio to a country station.

Breck had to fight the urge to pinch herself to make certain she wasn't dreaming. It couldn't possibly be real—riding along with Reese Thatcher in his pickup, on the way to spend Thanksgiving with his family—his confessing that he had wanted to kiss her that night at Marcelli's? Suddenly she wanted to throw her arms around him, kiss him square on the mouth, and thank him for being so wonderful! But she resisted and simply smiled at him as his hands drummed on the steering wheel in time to the music.

Eventually Reese led Breck to more comfortable lines of conversation, and the remaining trip out to Reese's parents' house was more at ease. Breck had watched the snow on the side of the roads getting deeper and deeper the more isolated the roads became. But just before eleven, Reese pulled up in front of a cozy-looking farmhouse—much newer than Breck had expected—and she felt a bit disappointed.

She'd been in the old ranch house out at El Costa Lotta. No one lived there now, but her Grandpa and Grandma McCall had lived their entire married lives. It was creaky, drafty, and needed a load of work. But it spoke of the past, of simpler times, of love, and of comfort, and Breck had adored it. She'd secretly hoped Reese's family home was a bit older—a bit more weathered. Still, the warm light that flooded the snowy ground outside the front window spoke of all the things farmhouses did—old or new.

No sooner had Reese helped Breck down from his pickup than Marjie Thatcher was racing out the front door, arms flung wide in greeting, jolly red apron strings flying at her back.

"Oh, there you are, you sweet girl!" Marjie greeted Breck, throwing her arms around her and hugging her tight. "And Reese, my baby," she cooed, releasing Breck and nuzzling into Reese's powerful embrace.

"You cooking already, Mom?" Reese asked.

"Of course!" Marjie said. Immediately she began to ramble, "Did you two have a nice trip up? What do you think of the drive, Breck? Reese said he was going to force you to bring some of your pumpkin pies. He says they're better than mine." All the time she rambled, Marjie smiled—looking like some sort of kitchen angel and smelling like flour, butter, and brown sugar.

"Oh…oh…I'm sure mine aren't nearly as—" Breck began.

"Nonsense," Marjie interrupted. "If Reese says they're better, then they are, and I can't wait to taste them."

Marjie put her arm around Breck's shoulders and began walking her toward the house. "Did Reese drive the speed limit? It scares me to death, these back roads. And in the winter…whew! Let me tell you, it's downright dangerous."

Reese smiled. Breck looked back at him over her shoulder as his mother pushed her along toward the house. She looked scared to death, and he chuckled—though feeling sympathy for her at the same time. She'd be fine once she was inside and everyone had gushed all over her. Breck would be fine with his family. But would he? He wondered if he had his head on straight enough to have come home for Thanksgiving and not make any rash decisions. He wondered if he had his head on straight enough to keep his hands off his adorable little assistant, Breck McCall. *Probably not*, he thought. And he chuckled, recalling the astonished look on her face when he'd told her he'd bargained with her friends to steal a kiss. He shook his head and swallowed the extra moisture that had flooded his mouth at the thought of kissing her. Four days out in the middle of nowhere? It could get interesting.

CHAPTER EIGHT

Mrs. Thatcher pushed Breck into a warm, cinnamon-scented home, filled with welcoming, smiling faces. Taking a quick inventory, she guessed everyone in Reese's family was there. Two little dark-haired girls sat in front of the fireplace playing with a pile of banged-up looking baby dolls. Two handsome young men with dark hair and striking resemblances to Reese stood with another young man with lighter hair. The three seemed to be steeped in conversation with an older, gray-haired man, lounging in a recliner nearby. And as Reese closed the door behind him, a very pretty young woman with Mrs. Thatcher's twinkling eyes squealed with excitement and threw her arms around Reese's neck.

"Oh, Reese!" the young woman laughed. "It's so good to see you." Then turning to look at Breck, she added, "And this must be Breck." She put a friendly arm around Breck's shoulders and hugged her briefly. "I'm Reese's sister, Katie. And Mom has told us all about you."

Breck felt like a new toy on Christmas morning.

She drew back slightly as Reese's father, brothers, and the light-haired young man made their way toward her. Stepping back—intimidated by the four men approaching—she heard Reese chuckle as she bumped into him.

"Don't worry, Breck," he whispered in her ear. "They won't eat you."

But Breck wasn't so certain. What had she been thinking when she'd accepted Mrs. Thatcher's invitation to visit?

"Nick Thatcher," one of the dark-haired men said, offering her his hand.

Breck accepted it and managed a timid, "Breck McCall," in response.

"Bobby Thatcher," the other young man with darker hair said.

He too offered Breck his hand, and she took it saying, "Nice to meet you."

"Keith Donaldson. I'm Katie's husband," the blonde man said, taking her hand as well. Breck managed another smile.

"And I'm Ben Thatcher, pretty girl," Reese's father said, moving to stand next to her and putting a strong arm around her shoulders. Breck smiled when she caught the scent of wind and hay as he hugged her. "And I'm sure you're just about plum overwhelmed with all us, now aren't you?" Ben Thatcher chuckled, and Breck noticed how much his chuckle sounded like Reese's.

"Katie and I are just whippin' up some barbeque

for lunch, kids," Mrs. Thatcher said. "Would you like to give us a hand in the kitchen, Breck?"

Breck sighed, relieved at being saved by the women, who no doubt understood her discomfort at being inspected from head to toe by the men in the room. "I'd love to," she said and smiled as Katie took her hand and led her away from the towering grove of Thatcher men.

"Reese, that there…that's worth livin' in the city for," she heard one of the men say in a lowered voice as she left. She heard the other sounds of men greeting each other, their low chuckles, and suddenly felt safer somehow—safer than she'd felt in years.

"We've just got some potato salad, baked beans, barbeque sandwiches, and chips," Marjie Thatcher said. "Thought we'd just pile each of them up a plate and slop 'em where they stand."

Even though she was quite overwhelmed with new people, an unfamiliar place, and being a stranger in her boss's family's home, Breck did begin to feel herself settling down. The Thatcher home was inviting— safe—the perfect haven for relaxation. As she entered the kitchen, she glanced around quickly, smiling at the quaint vintage decor and architecture. If it hadn't been for the microwave oven and other modern-day appliances, she could've sworn she'd stepped right into the 1940s. It was fabulous! The windows were dressed with yellow gingham valances and lace sheers, and a yellow tablecloth covered an old kitchen table. It was warm, fragrant, and beautiful.

"You wanna just plop a big ol' spoon of potato salad on each plate, Breck?" Katie asked, handing Breck the largest serving spoon she had ever seen.

"Sure," Breck said.

She began putting potato salad on each plate Mrs. Thatcher handed her, handing each plate in turn to Katie, who added a sandwich. When they'd finished and had deposited a plate heaping with good food into the hands of each man in the other room, Mrs. Thatcher, Katie, and Breck sat at the kitchen table to eat their lunch.

"Gotta slop the hogs before we can settle down to eat, don't we?" Katie giggled. Then, taking a sip from her cup of water, she asked Breck, "Did you have a nice drive down?"

"We did," Breck answered. "It seemed to go really fast too."

"Well, I don't know how," Marjie Thatcher sighed, "in that beat-up old thing Reese calls a pickup."

"Mom, you know he's got, like, 250,000 miles on that thing?" Katie said.

"I know it. He'll drive that thing 'til its guts fall out somewhere," Marjie remarked. "It probably jostled your kidneys clean to death," she added.

Breck giggled. "No. Not too badly."

"Makin' all that money and he still prefers to drive that old thing," Katie said. "Guess he's not as far from bein' home as he likes to think." There was a moment of quiet.

But not too long a moment before Marjie said, "So tell us about yourself, Breck."

Breck was feeling quite comfortable and asked, "What do you want to know?" It was a loaded question.

"Is my brother as good a kisser as he always bragged he was?" Katie asked.

Instantly Breck felt her face turn crimson. "I-I…"

Katie giggled and, aside to her mother, said, "Must be."

Marjie patted Breck on the hand, understanding her discomfort. "We tease a bit now and then, honey. You just let it roll off, and you'll be fine." Then, smiling warmly, she added, "Now, tell us…where did you grow up exactly?"

❦

Breck spent most of the afternoon in the yellow kitchen talking and laughing with Katie and her mother while Reese and the other men visited in the other room. Katie and Keith's little girls came in periodically for drinks of water, help with baby doll diapers, and cookies from grandma's cookie jar. But for the most part, the two toddlers stayed fairly well entertained by the men. Breck could remember being a small girl and sitting in front of the fire or in the old kitchen at El Costa Lotta—listening to the low, comforting hum of the adults as they visited. Those were some of the most secure, happy times of her life, and she relished the opportunity to be in a home permeated by a similar atmosphere.

Dinner came and went as well, and it wasn't until

afterward that she even had the chance to talk to Reese again. Yet just knowing he was there in the other room gave her comfort.

However, once dinner was over and Reese's brothers were busily doing up the dishes, Reese walked into the kitchen smiling. Breck noticed how relaxed he looked. The frown that often puckered his brow at work was gone.

"You wanna go with me to bust up the ice in the watering tanks?" he asked.

Breck smiled. "Sure," she said.

"Well, grab a coat 'cause, baby, it's cold outside," he said, taking her hand and pulling her to her feet. Instantly, his mother and sister broke into a verse of the popular song from the 1950s, whose title Reese had just quoted.

As they sang, Reese unexpectedly pulled Breck against him, leading her in a two-step as he joined his mother and sister in a chorus. Breck giggled, delighted by Reese's unexpected knowledge of one of her favorite old songs. When they'd finished their chorus, and it was quite well done, he took her hand and led her toward the door.

"We're going to bust up the troughs," Reese told his father as he helped Breck on with her coat.

"Yep. Bustin' up the troughs," Nick chuckled. "That's what Katie and Keith used to call it too." Breck felt herself burn a terrible blush. She was somewhat relieved as Reese made an attempt to defend her.

"Now, Nick," he began, "Breck's not used to such

teasing. You behave." Still, she saw him wink at his brother and continued to burn a blush.

Once outside, Reese shivered a low, "Brrrr!" and pulled his gloves on. "It's gonna get cold tonight. I hope you brought some warm pajamas."

"I did," Breck assured him.

"Come on then," he said, pulling her toward a four-wheel ATV parked nearby. Reese hopped on the four-wheeler, and it roared to life. "Hop on," he instructed, looking over his shoulder at her. "And hold on."

Breck smiled, delighted at the prospect of riding behind Reese on the four-wheeler and wrapping her arms tightly around him. Climbing on behind him, she put her arms around his waist and rested her chin on his shoulder. He smelled divine—like Speed Stick, chewing gum, and aftershave.

"Hang on," he told her again. In the next moment, they were riding through the night, the cold air stinging the tip of Breck's nose, but she didn't care. The air was fresh—still—alive with frost, and she was snuggling up against Reese Thatcher.

Not too far away from the house, they stopped. Reese climbed off the four-wheeler and told Breck to wait while he broke up the thin layer of ice that had formed over the top of the water in the tank. Even before he was finished, a group of cows began ambling their way toward the tank.

Climbing back on the four-wheeler, Reese let go another, "Brrr!" before adding, "They'd better tank up for the night. I'm not coming out before three in the morning. I want a good night's sleep."

"Three a.m. is a good night's sleep?" Breck asked.

Reese simply chuckled and started the four-wheeler toward the next watering tank.

That night Breck lay in bed staring over at the warmth of the wood-burning stove, still aglow with the dying embers of a fire. She was staying in Katie's old room, and the bed was soft and covered with well-worn quilts. Marjie had explained that in the morning Katie would be over to help prepare Thanksgiving dinner. Breck could imagine the excitement in the kitchen, the heavenly aromas.

She sighed, smiling as she listened to the low mumbles and chuckles coming from the room next door—the room where Reese was bunking in with Nick and Bobby. She wondered what they were talking about—family, friends, and the farm—maybe even her. It had been a wonderful day. Especially the hours spent in the pickup with Reese on the way to the farm—and the hour spent riding around with him as he broke up the ice in the water tanks. That had been blissful! She thought of the way he'd tweaked her cold nose after they'd finished—the way his eyes twinkled as he looked at his mother. Reese Thatcher had come home. And he'd brought Breck with him.

CHAPTER NINE

Thanksgiving morning on the Thatcher farm dawned cold, crisp, and frosty. The sun was trying to peek through the clouds, but Ben Thatcher said he was doubtful that it would succeed. Breck had awakened to the homey sounds of clanking dishes and the heavenly smell of frying bacon. She could hear the delighted giggles of little girls and figured Katie and her family had already arrived. She was thankful for the bathroom adjoining Katie's old room. It gave her privacy and enabled her to get ready for the day very quickly.

Stepping into the kitchen, she was met with the warmth and smells of a kitchen on Thanksgiving Day.

"Good morning," Katie said, smiling and giving Breck a quick hug. "Did the girls wake you?" she asked.

"Oh, no," Breck said. "The smell of bacon did."

"Well, now you sound like Reese," Marjie said, smiling at Breck. "That boy eats far too much of it, and if I don't cook enough, no one else will get a lick." Breck smiled as Reese's mother motioned for her to come over to where she stood at the stove frying the bacon. "Did you sleep well, honey?" Marjie asked her, hugging her with one arm as she slid the bacon around in the skillet with the other.

"Yes, thank you," Breck assured her. "And I'm sorry I slept so long."

"It's only six, Breck," Katie explained. "But Keith dropped me and the girls off on his way into town. I forgot the cranberries and had to send him to the store for some."

Breck looked around, but there wasn't a Thatcher man in sight. "Is everyone else still asleep?" she asked.

"Yep," Marjie said. "They went back to bed after breakin' up the ice in the tanks this mornin'."

Good. Breck hadn't wanted Reese to be up before her.

"But don't worry," Marjie added. "The smell of this bacon will have them up before long."

"Daddy ate one of your pumpkin pies for breakfast before he went out this morning, Breck," Katie said. "The whole thing! In one sitting!"

"I hope you don't mind, honey," Marjie said. "He loves pumpkin pie for breakfast on Thanksgiving morning and wanted to try one of yours."

"Oh, that's fine. I brought them for you," Breck told her.

"Well," Marjie began, "I did have a bite before he gobbled it down completely, and I do have to admit… Reese is right. Your pumpkin pie puts mine to shame." Marjie winked as Breck began to shake her head. "Oh, now don't go tryin' to be humble, Breck. Shout it from the rooftops. I'm pleased as punch about it."

Breck smiled, uncomfortable with the fact she might make a better pumpkin pie than the lady of the house.

Breck looked around then when she heard Reese mumble a "Good morning, ladies" as he entered the kitchen.

Her eyes widened as she beheld him wearing nothing but a pair of flannel pajama bottoms. The pajama bottoms were littered with cartoon character, but that wasn't what made her jaw go slack in astonishment. It wasn't even how adorable he looked with his hair tousled or the fact he rubbed his eyes with the heel of his hand like a tired toddler. What stunned her into shocked silence was the sight of him bare from the waist up! Quickly she closed her gaping mouth and turned around, going to stand closer to the stove next to Marjie—feigning interest in the frying bacon. Reese's torso was supreme in its muscular structure. His body looked more like a professional body sculptor's than a guy who worked an office job at an investigation firm.

"Happy Thanksgiving, Kate," she heard him tell his sister. Still, she didn't dare turn around and look at him again. It wasn't until she felt his arm—his bare arm—go around her shoulders as he stepped between her and his mother that she looked at him again. Even this time she only glanced up at him quickly.

"Happy Thanksgiving, Mom," he said, pulling his mother tight under one arm as he kissed her cheek affectionately.

"Breck," he said then, and she held her breath as he kissed her cheek too.

"Happy Thanksgiving, sweetie," his mother said, raising herself on her toes and kissing his whiskery cheek.

"Yes," Breck said as he looked down at her, smiling. "Happy Thanksgiving."

Reese inhaled deeply—exhaled a happy sigh. "How many pounds did you do, Mom?" he asked.

"Four, Reese. And that will be plenty, do you hear?" Marjie chuckled.

"That leaves three for everybody else to share," Reese said aside to Breck. Breck wished he'd take his arm from around her shoulders. Well, not really. She liked having him touch her. But it was making her terribly nervous. She wished he'd at least put a shirt on! Well, not really. But his state of undress was making her even more nervous.

"The ice in the tanks was an inch thick this morning, Mom," Reese said, releasing the two women and going to sit down at the table.

"It got pretty cold last night," Marjie said.

"Uncle Weese?" It was one of Katie's little girls—the oldest, Lizzy. Breck turned to watch the sweet child climb up onto Reese's lap and lock her hands at the back of his neck.

"What, sugar?" he asked, chuckling and twisting a lock of her hair around one finger for a moment.

"Why don't you have any babies?" Everyone laughed at Lizzy's sweet, innocent question.

Reese continued to chuckle as he answered, "Well, Lizzy...I don't have a wife. And a man needs a wife to have babies." The child looked at him and seemed pensive for a moment.

Then, to Breck's utter horror, Lizzy pointed to *her* and said, "I bet she could do it for you, Uncle Weese." Breck thought she might drop dead from the heat of the blush that rose to her cheeks. Marjie, Katie, and Reese erupted into laughter and giggles, but Breck remained red-faced.

"I bet she could," Reese managed to respond.

"I think she'd have pretty babies for you," the child prattled on.

"Yes, she would," Reese managed again—though his eyes were watering with mirth.

Breck wanted to dash from the room—escape the embarrassing situation. What could she possibly say? She felt Marjie pat her understandingly on the back, but it didn't really help to soothe her predicament.

And then the situation got worse as Reese said, "Why don't you ask her if she's up to it, sweetie?"

"What?" Breck gasped.

"Okay," Lizzy said, happily hopping down from her uncle's lap.

"Now, Reese, you quit," Marjie halfheartedly scolded.

Breck forced a smile at the little girl as she approached and took Breck's hand.

"Hey, lady," Lizzy began. Breck hunkered down so

the child could address her more easily. "You wanna have some babies for my Uncle Weese?"

Breck glanced up to Reese, who was bent over withholding his laughter. He winked at her—offering no salvation.

"I-I..." Breck stammered. What could she possibly say? "That's a big question, Lizzy, and I just got here yesterday," she said.

Reese burst into laughter, and Marjie and Katie were beside themselves.

Lizzy frowned for a moment. But then her face brightened. "Okay," she said, a disappointed sigh escaping her tiny lungs. "I'll tell him he has to wait a while longer." Breck breathed a sigh of relief herself and even managed a giggle when the child turned back to her and added, "Could you maybe have some kittens for me instead?"

The morning passed quickly with so much to be done to get such a big meal ready. Keith arrived with the cranberries, and Reese had followed him into the den, allowing Breck to survive the embarrassment she'd suffered at the hands of him and Lizzy. She'd even managed to keep breathing when he'd hugged her after breakfast—still bare-chested—telling her what a good sport she'd been.

Katie and Marjie were absolutely wonderful! They treated Breck as if they'd known her their whole lives—involving her in every aspect of preparing the meal. Once in a while throughout the morning, the three women would take what Marjie called "a cider break"—sit down at the kitchen table and sip a glassful of freshly made apple cider. They asked Breck questions, and she answered and asked her own. It was a beautiful, dreamy morning.

Furthermore, Breck had never seen such a perfectly prepared Thanksgiving dinner! The turkey was roasted to perfection and stuffed with fresh rosemary, thyme, and sage. Marjie Thatcher served her cornbread stuffing on the side, and it was unlike anything Breck had tasted since her Grandmother McCall's! Mashed potatoes, homemade gravy, candied yams, cranberry sauce, deviled eggs, black olives, green beans, and the lightest, sweetest dinner rolls Breck had ever eaten.

Reese's father had said the blessing before the meal and even thanked the Lord for their "beautiful addition, Miss Breck." However, the best part of the meal wasn't the antique china, the perfect food, or the friendly, loving conversation. It was the fact that Breck was seated next to Reese, who would put his arm across the back of her chair and rest his hand on her shoulder each time he leaned back to give his food time to settle.

Once in a while, he'd bend over and whisper something in her ear too. Something like, "Do you want me to get you anything else?" Or, "They're hilarious, aren't they?"

Breck simply cherished every moment spent at the table that day. She laughed with everyone else as Lizzy and Sarah put a large black olive on each of their fingers, popping them into their mouths one by one, then starting over. She smiled when Reese's father unfastened the button at the waist of his jeans to "allow for more fixin's," as he put it.

And when the feast was finished, she was amazed when Marjie and Katie led her into the living room while the men cleaned up before disappearing into the nearby den to hoot and holler over football. It was a day made of dreams come true, and Breck savored it as best she could.

Sitting in the living room on the sofa in front of the fireplace, Breck could see Marjie and Katie were as sleepy as she was.

Finally, Marjie said, "Time for a nap, girls…or we'll never make it to dessert."

"I'll have Keith watch the girls," Katie yawned. "Can I bunk in with you, Breck?"

"Of course," Breck said. How incredibly fast they'd accepted her. How incredibly comfortable she felt with them. It was strange—and wonderful!

"Breck? Breck?" his voice whispered again. Breck forced her eyes open to find Reese standing over her, smiling.

"Oh," she said. He put an index finger to his lips and pointed to Katie, still sleeping next to Breck on the bed. Sitting up carefully, she smiled at him.

"Do you want to go with me to bust up the ice again?" he asked. Breck's smile broadened, and she nodded. "Grab your shoes and a coat. I'll meet you outside." Breck nodded again and tried to hush the butterflies flapping around in her stomach.

It was already dark, and frost was again falling through a clear sky as they rode the four-wheeler from trough to trough to make sure the stock would be able to stay watered through the night.

Breck was surprised when Reese didn't head back to the house after checking on the horses but drove in an unfamiliar direction instead. Suddenly Breck could make out the shape of a house in the distance, silhouetted in the moonlight. There were no lights coming from it, however, and when Reese stopped the four-wheeler in front of it, she could tell that it was empty. Empty, but charming and beautiful!

"This is the house I grew up in," Reese told her as she stepped off the four-wheeler and followed him up the front porch stairs. It was hard to make out the exact architecture of the house in the dark, but Breck could tell it was old—an old Victorian-era house, complete with front bay window and two-story turret.

"We built the new house when I was about fourteen," Reese explained. "But...I still think of this one as home. I miss living in it." He pulled his keys from his pocket and sorted through them until he found the one he was looking for. Breck smiled—touched that he would still carry a key to his boyhood home.

"Want to see inside?" he asked, an expression of mischief blatant across his face.

"Certainly!" Breck assured him. She watched as he unlocked the door and pushed it open. It creaked to a stop, and Reese motioned for her to step inside.

Breck stepped cautiously into the old farmhouse,

and Reese stepped in after her, flipping a switch on the wall. Instantly the room before them was illuminated, and even though it stood empty now, somehow the echoes of times gone by—of lives lived in it—somehow the house still seemed welcoming and happy.

The house was the perfect example of an old farmhouse. The hardwood floors were worn but beautiful. The walls were once white and needed new paint badly, but what walls in an old farmhouse didn't? It smelled closed up, but not unpleasant like some old houses did. She imagined how cozy and warm a fire blazing in the nearby fireplace would be.

Reese smiled and lowered his voice, as if revealing a great secret. "Fifth, sixth, and seventh stairs up squeak." He pointed to the staircase that led from the front or parlor area up to the second floor. "Mom and Dad always knew when one of us was trying to sneak out or in…'cause those three stairs would squeak, and if we tried to skip them and hop up to the eighth, the thud was too loud." Breck smiled at the image of three teenage farm boys trying to sneak to bed after having missed curfew.

"That bay window is beautiful!" Breck exclaimed. "A perfect Christmas tree spot," she mumbled, speaking her thoughts out loud.

"That's what my mom always said," Reese chuckled. "Every year she complains about not having a good spot for the tree in the new house."

"Well," Breck said, going over to stand in the bay window area, "it is the most important part of a house, you know." She smiled when Reese shook his head, obviously amused by the priorities of some women. She turned and looked out the window to the clean, unmarred winter scene beyond. Snow and trees—just snow and trees—no other buildings as far as she could see—frost sifting through the air, sparkling like glitter in the moonlight.

"Many are the Christmas Eves that I stood just there, peering out the window, hoping to see Santa and his sleigh fly by," Reese chuckled.

"It's the perfect spot to watch for him," Breck said. She sighed, enraptured by the entire moment.

"This house," Reese said, coming to stand beside her and following her gaze out the window into winter, "it's…it's…"

"Magical," Breck finished for him. A strange tingling sensation caused her to shiver.

"You cold?" he asked, having noticed her shivering.

"A little," she lied.

"We can go, if you want to," he said. "Mom will have hot chocolate waiting, and we can warm you up."

Breck nodded, even though she paused in wanting to leave the house. Somehow, she'd fallen in love with it, as well as the boy who grew up embraced in its loving walls.

"So," Reese's dad began, "tell me about this girl."

Reese feigned ignorance as he sat on the sofa next to his dad's lounge chair. He smiled as he watched the fire burn and heard his sister, mother, and Breck giggling over a game of rummy in the other room. He knew his father wouldn't be deterred, but it was worth a try.

"What do you mean?" he asked.

Ben Thatcher chuckled. "You know what I mean, boy." He leaned back in his armchair and waited for an answer.

Reese grinned, shaking his head. "She's my assistant at work."

"So you're seducin' your secretary, huh?" his father said.

"It's been done before, Pop," Reese said, smiling.

"That it has, son. That it has." Ben sighed—a sign that he was finally relaxing for the day. "What are your plans then?" he asked.

Reese shrugged. "You mean plans for life…or for Breck?"

"Both. I reckon they're about to become one and the same."

Reese chuckled. "Pop…she's just—"

"She ain't *just* nothin', son," his father interrupted. "Come on now…tell me. What does she put you in mind of?"

Reese was trapped, and he knew it. Once his father got something stuck in his brain, there was no deterring him until he was satisfied. He could spot a lie a mile away too. So there was nothing left to do but 'fess up.

"She puts me in mind of…of changing careers, for one thing," Reese admitted. "I'm tired of dealing with criminals, infidelity…basically all the crap involved with my job. Not that there are many jobs where a man doesn't have to deal with it. Just that..."

"You're finally rememberin' that although there're a few piles of manure out in the barn...they ain't as ugly as what you're dealin' with at Wilson."

Reese nodded. "Still...somebody has to shovel it, Pop. Somebody has to fight for the good people who need help."

"Somebody does, Reese. But that don't mean it has to be at Wilson." His dad leaned forward—a serious scowl on his face. "Ranchin', farmin', and the like...it's hangin' on by the skin of its teeth, Reese. Everybody knows it. But as long as someone's fightin' to keep it... this country won't go completely to the dogs." His dad sighed again, and Reese didn't balk the argument he'd heard so many times. For one thing, he agreed. "And...I'll tell you this," Ben added. "You wouldn't be keepin' such a tight-fisted hold on that old house and the acreage you own here if you didn't know it."

Reese nodded. "I'll admit to you, Pop. Lately...I've been thinking about...about..."

"Just say it, son. You ain't gonna explode for sayin' it out loud," Ben urged.

Reese drew in a deep breath and admitted, "I've been thinking about...about coming back out here, fixing up the old house, running a few cattle..."

"It's the girl that got you thinkin'?" his father asked. Reese shrugged—but his father knew him too well. "Good! I like a girl who makes a man reevaluate his life. And she's a pretty little thing. Comes from good stock too."

Reese smiled. "You like her 'cause she's got horses in her blood," Reese chuckled.

His father smiled. "I like her 'cause she's gettin' under your skin."

"She ain't getting under my skin, Pop," Reese lied, standing to leave.

"Oh, she's under your skin all right. Never known you to bring a girl home for Thanksgiving, local or otherwise," Ben said, yawning.

"Mom invited her, remember," Reese said.

"And you invited your mom out to dinner that night, boy," his father countered. "And besides…I saw you takin' her out to the old place."

"I just wanted to show her where I grew up," Reese told him.

"Hm-hmm," his father chuckled. "That's why I took your mother out there the first time too."

Breck couldn't sleep. Even by midnight she was still wide awake, all the wonders of the day replaying over and over and over in her mind—that morning in the kitchen, Reese's kissing her on the cheek, Lizzy's baby questions, the beautiful dinner, and the evening ride out with Reese to the old family home. It was marvelous, and all Breck could think about was the wonder of it all and how she would ever go back to everyday life. Even watching the family's favorite Christmas movie that evening before everybody went to bed. It was perfect! She covered her mouth to muffle her giggles as she remembered Reese's father wiping the tears of joy from his cheeks as the little boy in the movie was daydreaming about getting a BB gun for Christmas. All of it, the entire day—all of them—it had been perfect. And Reese! Reese had been perfect! Perfectly cute in his cartoon character pajamas—perfectly gorgeous with his shirt off—perfectly attentive and flirtatious. And there were still three days to go!

Getting to sleep soon was not an option, and Breck knew it. Perhaps a piece of pumpkin pie would do the trick. Yes—carbohydrates always helped relax her.

Quietly, she stepped into the hallway, peering right, then left to make sure no one else was about. On her way to the kitchen, however, she smiled as she saw the dying embers in the fireplace burning orange and inviting. Maybe a few minutes in front of the fire would find her eyes heavy.

Breck sat down on the sofa in front of the fire. She could still feel its warmth—even for its ending. She smiled, imagining what the next day would bring. Marjie had explained that it was "Christmas tree hunting day!" The family always went out for a bit of snow play and to get a Christmas tree the day after Thanksgiving.

"Who wants to go shopping and mess with the crowds?" Marjie had said. "The day after Thanksgiving… we do our tree."

Breck was excited about the prospect. For one thing, she was certain it was quite the event to behold.

"Sneaking out of bed, eh?" Reese whispered.

Breck startled and put her hand to her chest to still the wild thumping of her heart at the sound of Reese's voice.

"You scared me nearly to death!" she told him in a whisper. Quickly she made sure her pajama top was buttoned all the way up. The top buttonhole was stretched, and it sometimes came unfastened. Breck was suddenly very self-conscious about her all too casual attire. But her state of dress in which she appeared was soon driven from her mind when she noted that Reese again wore nothing but pajama bottoms.

Plopping down beside her on the sofa, Reese stretched his legs out in front of him, crossed his ankles, and began eating handfuls of bacon from the bag of bacon bits he'd obviously snitched from the kitchen.

Breck felt her eyebrows raise, accompanying her amused smile as she watched him eat his bacon bits.

Reese smiled and winked at her, holding the bag out toward her and asking, "Bacon?"

Breck paused for a moment and then nodded, holding out her hand. He poured a nice fistful into her hand.

"Don't worry. Eat as much as you want," he told her. "There's tons more out in the freezer. And they're real bacon. Not that imitation junk."

Breck smiled, amused at his addiction to breakfast meat.

"I'm glad Mom invited you and made me come home…and thanks for coming," he said.

"Me too," Breck admitted in a whisper. "Thanks for bringing me," she told him, glancing down at her lap.

"Thanks for bringing *me*," he told her. "It was time I came home."

Breck smiled at him. He belonged here. She felt it.

"So, tell me about this book," he said, dumping some bacon directly from the bag into his mouth.

"What do you mean?" she asked. His nearness was unsettling. Breck felt an uncomfortable warmth begin in her stomach and fan out through her body. "What book?"

"This book that has this highwayman guy in it that you like so much." He grinned at her. "I mean, you must really like it for your friends to go to all that trouble in finding a guy to dress up like this highwayman for your birthday and all."

Not this again. She'd never hear the end of it— from Reese or her friends. Breck blushed, and the warmth spreading through her body worried her. What if she actually began to perspire from it? She looked at him for a moment—tried not to notice the perfectly sculpted muscles of his chest and stomach—tried not to think about how even more handsome he was with his hair tousled, wearing flannel pajama bottoms covered in cartoon characters.

He tipped his head back, shaking the last few bacon bits out of the bag and into his mouth before smiling at her and saying, "Come on. Tell me about the book."

Breck knew she was cornered. There would be no

changing the subject. But after Lizzy's questions about babies—could anything be worse?

"There's really nothing much to tell," she lied. "It's just a silly book that I've always liked."

"Well," he urged, "tell me about it. What's the title?"

She felt so overheated! However, she sighed heavily and figured there was no escape. After all, he deserved to know about it since he did go to all that trouble on her birthday. Besides, hadn't he told her one of his deepest secrets on the drive down?

"Well...it's pretty cliché really," she began. "It's called *The Highwayman of Tanglewood*." He nodded, set the empty bacon bits bag on the floor by the sofa, and looked at her expectantly, indicating that she should continue.

Taking hold of the hem of her pajama top and twisting it nervously, she continued, "It's about this guy who does the Robin Hood thing, sort of. You know, he dresses up like a highwayman and robs rich, criminal-type aristocrats and gives the money to the poor. And when he's dressed up like the Highwayman, he keeps running into this one girl...who of course is enamored of him."

"Enamored?" Reese interrupted, smiling.

Breck tensed as Reese scooted closer to her on the sofa. "You know...she was bewitched, captivated... enchanted by him," she explained, brushing a stray strand of hair from her cheek.

He smiled at her. "I know what it means. I just thought it was cute…the way you used the word."

Breck felt more heat rise to her cheeks as Reese rested his arm on the sofa behind her shoulders. He was flirting with her! Surely she was imagining it—the mischievous twinkle in his eye, the way he grinned almost seductively at her. The day had been too busy—filled with too many other people for her to have a chance to get nervous in his presence most of the time. But now—now that they were alone in the dead of night…

As her heart began to hammer hard within her chest with the thrill of his nearness, Breck prattled on, "Anyway…the girl always finds herself in his path. And of course he's quite the rogue…flirting with her, always saving her from peril…"

"He's a rogue?" he said, smiling. "Well…he would be, wouldn't he? Being a highwayman and all."

Breck's entire body broke into goose bumps as she felt Reese's hand leave the sofa back, slip beneath her hair at the back of her neck, and come to rest there. She looked at him quickly, denying the urge to throw herself against him and kiss him straight on the mouth.

"Anyway," she continued nervously, "it turns out she knows him when he's not dressed as the Highwayman too, of course. They're acquainted in real life as well, you see…"

"Kind of like the whole secret identity thing, right?" he asked, lowering his voice and weaving a strand of her hair through his fingers.

"Yeah," Breck choked out. She looked away from him and tried to focus on the light of the dying embers in the fireplace—tried to ignore the way his fingers kept caressing her neck as he toyed with her hair. "You see, she's a maid in the house that he…" But she stopped abruptly as she realized how desperately she did not want to reveal the heroine in the story actually worked as maid in the Highwayman's own house.

But it was too late. She heard Reese chuckle, and then he said, "Ohhh. I get it. He was her boss."

Breck couldn't help but smile and glanced down to where her hands were more violently twisting the bottom of her top. "Yeah," she admitted.

"I'm *your* boss," he needlessly reminded her.

"You are," was all she could force from her throat.

He chuckled again and said, "You've got some impish friends, Miss Breck."

"Believe me, I know it," she admitted, still afraid to look at him—still afraid that he could hear the mad hammering of her heart—sense her unbearable attraction to him.

"Does it all work out in the end?" he asked, lowering his voice as he moved even closer to her. She was tucked securely under his arm now and had to remind herself to breathe.

"Yes," she whispered.

"Does he seduce her into—" he whispered.

"No, no, no," Breck interrupted. "He's a gentleman. He…"

"But he does kiss her a lot, right?" he whispered.

"Yes," Breck managed.

He leaned toward her, his lips hovering just a breath away from the flesh of her neck just below her left ear, and whispered, "I've always wanted to kiss you, you know."

"Y-you have kissed me," she reminded him without turning toward him. She was going to fly apart! Explode into a million tiny particles! She could feel his breath on her neck—sense his lips just above her skin.

"That doesn't count," he whispered. "The first time you thought I was Marty Sprague," he reminded her. "The second time was after dinner with my mother. Neither one counts."

"What?" she asked. He just chuckled. "And anyway, I knew who you were that night at Marcelli's," she countered, trying to steady her emotions. "You'd already taken your mask off."

Her heart pounded so fiercely in her chest that she wondered if it might just burst through! She hoped he couldn't tell that she was having trouble regulating her breathing.

She heard him chuckle again. "Why are you so nervous?" he asked.

"I'm...I'm not nervous," she lied, twisting her pajama top even more violently.

He took her chin in one hand and turned her face to his. Instantly, her gaze fell to his delicious, grinning mouth. She felt warm moisture flood her own as she thought of his lips on hers.

"You're a liar," he told her. "You're ready to jump up and run."

"It's just that..." she stammered. "I've never...had anyone just tell me...just talk to me about it..."

"Well, if it's making you nervous to talk about it," he whispered as he lowered his head toward hers, "then I won't."

Breck gasped a moment before Reese kissed the corner of her mouth softly. Slowly, lingeringly, he kissed her upper lip, then her lower lip. Breck tried to draw in a quick breath, knowing she would black out if she couldn't find a way to start breathing again. But nature has a way of keeping a person alive, even during the most intense moments of their lives, and when Reese kissed her lower lip again, taking her face in his hands a moment before his mouth took hers fully, Breck found her body relaxed enough to breath—at least for a moment. His kisses didn't remain soft for long. In the next moment, she felt passion rise in him, his mouth working a spell of bewitching ecstasy with hers as hot, deep kisses erupted between them.

Reese Thatcher had had a lifetime of practice at impassioned kissing! It was the only explanation Breck's fevered mind could conjure for such a skill possessed by a man in kissing. The way his lips, his mouth worked to draw passion from hers while simultaneously taking her breath away over and over—it just wasn't normal!

Another moment and Breck knew she would be lost, unable to stop kissing him. So rather abruptly she pulled away from him, placing her hand over her mouth to keep herself from going back as she tried to catch her breath.

Breck had been kissed before, but none of the other kisses had undone her so completely. None had threatened to break her heart so thoroughly as Reese's did. And she knew why—because she loved him. And yet the world was the way it was, and most men and women didn't save the ultimate intimacy for marriage. But Breck *was* saving it, and it was impossible to imagine a man like Reese Thatcher—gorgeous, fun, strong, seductive—would not be expecting more than kisses from such a situation. All at once, she wondered if he'd agreed to bring her home simply because he thought he might benefit from the deal. But surely— surely he was a better man than most.

Breck had never feared such a situation with Reese because she'd never entertained the thought that it could actually happen. But it was happening! And he was a gorgeous, no doubt passionate man. Her stomach churned at the thought of the other women he'd probably known in his life.

Breck felt tears welling in her eyes as Reese asked, "What's the matter?" He placed a hand to her cheek and caressed her lips with his thumb. "Am I that bad?"

Breck looked at him to find him grinning at her—an expression of understanding on his face. But understanding from a man in this day and age would be too much to expect. Especially a man like Reese, who could, no doubt, have his way with any woman he chose.

Still holding back tears and trying to stall the ache that had begun to throb in her heart, Breck shook her head, smiled, and whispered, "I think you know you're not bad."

"Then what's the matter, Miss Breck? Can you think of a better way to spend your Thanksgiving vacation than making out with your boss?" he whispered, kissing her cheek tenderly.

Breck breathed a giggle. He was so charming—so refreshingly blunt. "No. I mean..." she stammered, embarrassed.

"Then what?" he asked. "I know you don't have a boyfriend. I asked your skinny blonde friend."

Breck looked to him, rather astonished. "What?"

He smiled at her, brushed her cheek with the back of his hand, and said, "Just tell me what's wrong. You're holding back from me. I can tell." He ran his index finger the length of her nose and said, "I want to kiss you, Breck. And I'm pretty sure that you want to kiss me back. So what's stopping you?"

Breck swallowed hard—held onto her tears. In truth, she wondered for a moment if her conviction would stand where Reese was concerned. Was she too in love with him to resist if he decided to try and lead her down the hallway to his bedroom? And yet she knew she was strong enough—strong enough to break her own heart and push him away with the truth.

"It's just that...will you still want to kiss me after I tell you that I don't..." she stammered. Reese would turn away too. Just like every other man she'd dated.

And Reese was different; her feelings for him were different. It would break her heart to lose a chance to win him for her own.

"After you tell me that you don't what?" he prodded, softly. He took her hand in his and raised it to his lips, kissing it firmly. When she still paused, he said, "Just tell me, Breck."

Breck looked down at her mangled pajama top hem and, taking a deep breath, said, "After I tell you that I don't...that I'm an old-fashioned girl. That I don't..." she stammered in a whisper.

She heard Reese sigh and looked up to see him smiling at her. Again he caressed her tender lips with one thumb as he held her face in his hand.

"Oh, I see," he said. She looked away shyly as he continued, "When you tell me that you're an old-fashioned girl...and kissing is as far as you go, right?"

Breck closed her eyes and nodded. Two tears escaped and traveled slowly down her cheeks. But she gasped when next Reese pulled her into his arms—kissing her neck several times in succession, sending goose bumps erupting over Breck's arms and legs. It was only natural that she return his embrace, and the warmth of his skin felt fabulous beneath her palms.

"Well, guess what, Miss Breck?" he whispered as he kissed the top of her head. Then he released her from his embrace, took her face between his powerful hands, and, as she looked up at him through tear-filled eyes, said, "There are still a few old-fashioned boys around."

"What?" she breathed. He couldn't be serious! Surely he was teasing her. Still, hope rose in her bosom like a phoenix from the ashes as she searched his eyes for any sign of deceit. She found none.

"Just kiss me, Breck," he whispered. "You can trust me." And she believed him. She could see the sincerity in his eyes.

"Okay," she whispered as his head descended toward hers. She felt fear and heartache evaporate from her soul—thrilled at the knowledge his kiss would be hers again. Softly he kissed her upper lip—teasingly kissed her lower lip twice in succession. He nearly took her mouth with his, pausing only a breath before their lips would've met.

"However," he began in a low, alluring, entirely seductive tone, "that doesn't mean that I wouldn't want to or be very tempted to…to help you have a litter of kittens for Lizzy if the opportunity presented itself," he said. "It just means…that I wouldn't."

She smiled and melted into his arms as his mouth captured hers in a kiss borne of dreaming.

CHAPTER TEN

Everyone at the Thatcher farm awoke, rose, and dressed early the next morning. Breck had enjoyed heavenly dreams—thanks to Reese's delicious affections the night before. She enjoyed helping Marjie whip up a quick breakfast of pancakes (and, of course, bacon) before Katie, Keith, and the girls arrived. As soon as they did, everyone in the family piled into various beat-up pickup trucks and were off on the "adventure of the year," as Marjie had called it.

Every year on the day after Thanksgiving, the Thatcher family (now accompanied by the Donaldson family) spent all morning playing in the snow: sledding, inner tubing, snowmobiling—the works. Then, by about noon, they'd take a break, warm up with some hot cocoa and muffins, and set out to find the Thatcher family Christmas tree. Since Katie had married Keith, there was twice the fun, for there were two trees to hunt down.

Mrs. Thatcher had packed extra snow boots, coats, hats, and mittens, and now Breck found herself sitting next to Reese in his pickup, his brother Nick beside her, on her way to her first snow play day in years.

"Wooo whooo!" Nick shouted, a huge smile lighting up his face. "I love the snow!"

Reese chuckled. "We're heading up to Doe Ridge, Breck," he explained. "Great hills for sleds and tubes!"

Breck nodded, rather nervous. It was so strange, all of it—sitting next to Reese in the pickup, his acting like nothing out of the ordinary had passed between them the night before. She still had goose bumps cropping up now and again just at the memory! But he seemed as relaxed as ever he had been since they'd arrived, and so she tried to act as normal as she could.

"Did Reese ever tell you about the time he ran his ride into a barbed-wire fence, Breck?" Nick asked.

"He told me that it happened but didn't offer any details," Breck answered.

"Well," Nick began, "ol' Reese nearly lost his movie-star looks that day, I'll tell you."

"Shut up," Reese whined at his brother.

But Breck was interested. "Really?" she prodded.

"Yep," Nick continued. "We were out in Simpson's Woods…out east of the old house, remember, Reese?"

Reese nodded and said, "Oh, I remember."

"We were riding fast…really pushing the limit on Pop's snowmobiles," Nick explained. "Rrrrrrr! Rrrrrrrr!" Breck smiled as the young man made snowmobile sound effects and held his hands out in front of him to simulate where his hands would've been on the handles of a snowmobile. "Yep! We were flyin'!"

"We were, weren't we?" Reese smiled at the daring memory.

"We were flyin' so fast and racing, of course," Nick said.

"Of course," Breck said. She could just imagine it—two farm kids out on their father's snowmobiles, mortality being something that only other people had to deal with. She remembered how her cousins out at El Costa Lotta behaved.

"And the sun was so bright on the snow that day. Remember, Reese?" Nick asked.

"Ohhh, yeah." Reese did remember.

"Anyway," Nick continued, "we're flyin' along, me and Tom and Reese…and, well, you know what a maniac Reese is, right, Breck?"

"Sure," Breck agreed, though she hoped he'd settled down a bit since he was nineteen.

"All of a sudden, I see Reese go flying out of the seat of his ride! It looked like he'd hit an ejection button or something! Then I saw the fence—the snowmobile got all caught up in it. Well, by the time we got over to him, it looked like he'd been starring in some sick slasher movie, you know?" Breck wrinkled her nose and shivered a bit at the thought of Reese so terribly hurt. "Fortunately for the ladies, the worst damage was across his chest…like, just below his collar bone. Have you seen the scars?" Nick asked.

"No," Breck answered, trying hard to remember if she'd noticed any scars on Reese when he'd been prancing around shirtless the morning and night before.

"That's right!" Nick explained. "'Cause we took him all the way to Denver! They had a good plastic surgeon come in and stitch him up. He's still got the one scar on his forehead that's pretty ugly though. Show her, Reese."

Reese didn't pause but reached up, pulling his hair off his forehead.

"See? Right there at his hairline," Nick pointed out. Breck did see a scar about four inches long at the point on Reese's head where Nick had indicated.

"I was wearing some good goggles that day too," Reese told her, "or else that wire would've clean poked my eyes out or cut right through them to my brain."

Breck wrinkled her nose and shivered, horrified again at the thought of Reese in such peril.

"Three-hundred and twenty-three stitches total. Right, Reese?" Nick asked.

"Yep," Reese confirmed.

"But we were flyin' that day, weren't we?" Nick chuckled.

"Dang right!" Reese laughed, meeting Nick's upheld hand with a slap from his own.

"No barbed wire where we're headed today, right?" Breck asked. She hadn't enjoyed the retelling of the story as much as the men had.

Both men laughed, and Nick put a comforting arm around her shoulder. "No. But there are a lot of good places to go for a roll in the snow…if you know what I mean."

Breck blushed as Reese said, "You got that right!" and handed his brother another high-five.

"Mmm mmm," Reese whispered, leaning over and seeming to inhale the scent of Breck's hair. "I can't wait to roll down a hill with you, baby!"

"What?" Breck exclaimed, simultaneously blushing from head to toe.

Nick and Reese both chuckled—amused at her reaction.

"Nothing like making out in the snow," Nick sighed.

"What?" Breck gasped, blushing deeper.

Reese chuckled. "Don't worry, Breck. I'll make sure everything else stays warm too…not just your mouth."

Again Nick and Reese high-fived over Breck's head. She couldn't believe how forward he was being. He always seemed so guarded at work. But then again, he did work with women like Jamie Reynolds.

Breck smiled as Nick and Reese began talking about other terrifying adventures they'd had as youth. It was wonderful to hear them talking, laughing, enjoying each other's company. But mostly she smiled at the prospect of Reese kissing her in the snow. It did sound delicious!

And it was! The morning of playing in the snow with Reese and his family was incredible—from watching Lizzy and Sarah squeal with delight as their Uncle

Bobby sent their sled racing down a five-foot incline to hearing Ben's and Marjie's laughter as their inner tubes collided on Doe Ridge. But most of all, it was the moments when Reese would suddenly tackle Breck (however gently) and roll her down a snowy hill, capturing her mouth in a molten kiss drenched with playful passion, that were Breck's favorites!

She'd watched Reese frolicking with his family—awed at his easy manner, his careless smile and laughter. She'd return his kisses, embraces, and smiles, enraptured by his untroubled ease and confidence. And his family—they didn't seem at all surprised by his behavior toward her! In fact, they acted as if—as if they'd expected it all along. It was wonderful! Breck felt as if she were carried away in a movie or a dream… some surreal fantasy that couldn't possibly be actually happening. And yet—it was! And it was wonderful!

After a quick snack and some hot hot chocolate, everyone formed two lines—one behind Marjie and one behind Katie. It seemed the matrons of the family were the leaders on the trek into the woods to find the perfect Christmas trees. It wasn't an easy walk either. Apparently Marjie and her daughter were not women to be pampered into settling for second best when it came to Christmas trees. It took nearly two hours before trees were found that received everyone's approval—including Marjie's and Katie's. It was delightful, and after Ben, Reese, Nick, Bobby, and Keith had chopped, sawed, dragged, and loaded the wonders of nature into the back of Ben's and Keith's pickups, everyone else hopped in the with the trees for the ride home. Everyone, that is, except Breck—she wanted to ride in the cab of Reese's truck with him.

With Nick in the back of Keith's pickup with his nieces, Breck was left alone with Reese in his. Initially, she'd jumped in on the passenger's side. But Reese had quickly taken hold of her arm, coaxing her to sit right next to him.

"You're a bit different out here," Breck told him as they drove back toward the farmhouse. She laughed as she watched Lizzy and Sarah bobbing around in the back of the pickup, holding on to their beloved Christmas tree—protecting it from harm as their daddy drove it home.

"I suspect I'm a lot more than a bit different out here, Breck," Reese admitted. "Do you like me more… or less?" he asked.

"The same," Breck told him. And it was true. She loved him when they were at work or out finding his mother's perfect Christmas tree.

"So," he began, the familiar grin of mischief spreading across his face, "all these months we've been working together…you would've let me kiss you all along?"

Breck blushed and took a chance, revealing, "Yes."

"You mean, I've wasted all this time…afraid you'd think I was a…a…"

"Philanderer?" she finished for him.

He laughed. "I can't even say that word…but yes!"

Breck shrugged. "You're Reese Thatcher," she told him, simply.

"So?" he said. He was sweet. He truly wasn't aware of the effect he had on women—people in general, for that matter. When she didn't respond, he added, "And to think of all the trouble I went to tricking you into it....the Highwayman of Tanglewood. Oh, brother."

But Breck smiled and snuggled against him as he put his arm around her shoulders. In that moment, it truly seemed that all her dreams were about to come true.

Breck leaned back against Reese's chest. She could feel his firm muscles against her back as he wrapped his arms around her, folding them across her waist. Sighing heavily, she glanced at the fire, burning low but still burning in the fireplace. The sofa was soft, Reese was strong, and the tree...the tree was beautiful!

It had taken the entire evening for the Thatcher family and Breck to decorate the Christmas tree. Breck smiled as she remembered the way Marjie had handed out orders to Ben as he awkwardly wrapped the lights around the noble fir.

"Don't tell me how to put the lights on, woman!" Ben had grumbled. "I've been doing it for thirty years, haven't I?"

Once the lights were on, Marjie opened two boxes of old, yet still shiny, glass ornament balls—red and gold. Everyone helped hang these, and Breck again smiled when she caught Marjie rearranging them all a bit.

"My boys just don't quite have the eye for it, you know," she had whispered aside to Breck. "But they try."

After all the colored balls were perfectly arranged, it was time for the specialty ornaments. Marjie had several boxes full of them. There were little wooden soldiers made out of old-fashioned clothespins—various reindeer, snowmen, nutcrackers, and Santas—tiny wooden mice with beds or nests made from small matchboxes or walnut halves. There were nativities and stars, even real candy canes. Each ornament seemed to mean something special to one or the other of Marjie's sons. She explained that she'd made or purchased a new ornament for each of her children every Christmas since they were born.

"Katie took hers when she got married and hangs them on her own tree now," she told Breck. "I wish one of my boys would get married. Then I'd have some room for some new things." She winked at Breck, and Breck blushed—flattered but uncomfortable with Marjie's implication.

The final tradition before the tree would be completed with the addition of silver strands of icicles was the moment when Marjie handed each of her sons their new ornament. Breck found she was suddenly overcome by emotion as she watched this tradition unfold.

Bobby took the small box his mother handed to

him and chuckled when he withdrew a small snowman ornament. He thanked his mother, kissing her on the cheek and winking at his father, who sat in his lounge chair, obviously amused by the proceedings.

Nick's box contained a small reindeer made out of clothespins, and he too thanked his mother before finding a place for it on the tree.

Reese's ornament was a nutcracker, and it was then Breck realized one theme of the tree.

"I loved nutcrackers as a kid, so Mom always gets me a new one. Don't you?" Reese explained, lovingly kissing his mother's cheek, then finding a place for his newest nutcracker.

"And this is for you, honey," Marjie said, holding out a small box to Breck.

Breck was stunned. Already she'd had a hard time withholding her tears—the entire evening was so wonderful—but this was too much.

"I hope it's all right," Marjie said as Breck took the box in her trembling hands.

"You didn't have to—" Breck began.

"Oh, nonsense!" Marjie interrupted. "Now open it. See if you like it at all."

Reese was smiling understandingly at her, and Breck heard Ben chuckle from his seat in his lounge chair.

Breck gasped as she pulled the fragile ornament from the box.

"I thought of you the moment I saw it!" Marjie exclaimed.

Breck tried to keep the tears from spilling onto her cheeks, for there in her hand was the prettiest little porcelain doll Breck had ever seen. The little doll's head was covered in brown ringlets, a lace dress was her fashion, and in her lap she held, of all things, a tiny pumpkin!

"It's beautiful!" Breck whispered. "I can't believe you've gone to all this trouble."

Marjie giggled with excitement. "It was no trouble." Then hugging Breck, she said, "Now...find a place on the tree for your dolly."

"On *this* tree?" Breck asked. Surely Reese's mother wasn't inviting her to hang her ornament on Reese's family tree!

"Of course!" Marjie exclaimed. "After all, don't you want to see her there when you come back for Christmas?"

"Christmas?" Breck asked. She heard Reese chuckle.

"You're about as subtle as a train wreck, Mom," he said.

"Of course, Christmas! Reese says your family will still be away. That means you can come and spend it with us!" Marjie jingled.

"I-I couldn't possibly," Breck tried to argue.

"Nonsense," Marjie said. "Now put your dolly on, and we'll finish up with the icicles. Ben? Are you going to help?"

"I suppose you'll skin me if I don't," Ben mumbled, groaning as he exited his lounge chair.

There was nothing she could do. Carefully, Breck

hung the beautiful little doll on a tender branch of the Thatcher family Christmas tree.

"Perfect!" Marjie exclaimed. "And now you *have* to come for Christmas!"

Breck looked to Reese, who winked at her and nodded. She knew she'd still have to argue the point for appearance's sake—but could it be? Could she really be coming home with Reese again? And for Christmas?

"Mom helped us kids to make those the year I was twelve," Reese was saying. Breck pulled her attention back to the moment at hand. He chuckled, "Those danged old clothespin soldiers. I remember how mad she got when Nick, Bobby, and I started dipping toothpicks in the red paint and gluing them onto the soldiers' chests so it looked like they'd been stabbed." He laughed again. "Katie started crying and telling Mom that we were going to ruin Christmas, so Mom made us start all over."

Breck looked at the little clothespin soldiers with their black pom-pom hats. She could just imagine what a mess the Thatcher boys had made of their mother's craft project that year.

Oh, the tree was so beautiful, twinkling in the darkness of the room. The glass ornaments and silver icicles on the tree caught all the colors of the tree lights, casting color on the walls and ceiling, making pure magic of the moment. The only other light in the room was coming from the fire in the hearth, and it sent the comforting aroma of cedar wafting through the warm air, soothing the night even more. Reese's mother had left her Christmas music playing on the stereo, and the soft, restful sound of Nat King Cole's honey-coated voice singing a familiar Christmas song completed the atmosphere of contentment in the room.

"We'll have to leave the Tuesday before Christmas to come out," Reese said unexpectedly. "And early too, 'cause the snow is usually pretty bad out here by then. It'll take us longer to make the drive."

"I cannot possibly come here for Christmas, Reese. It's…it's rude," Breck told him, hoping he would argue.

He did. "It's not rude, and you are coming. And besides, I promised Mom," he told her.

"Do *you* want me to come home with you for Christmas?" she couldn't help asking. Everything seemed so perfect—so perfectly dreamy—too dreamy to be real, somehow. She worried that perhaps it was only Reese's mother who wanted her to come out to the farm for Christmas.

Reese chuckled and took hold of Breck's chin, turning her face toward his. "Who do you think planted the thought in her mind?"

Breck smiled up at him. He was wonderful! Could this all really be happening to her? And what would happen when they got back to the city? To work? To the real world?

In the next moment, Reese bent, kissing her upper lip. His kiss lingered on her lower lip and lingered there once more before he turned her in his arms and took her mouth with his own. Instantly Breck's heart seemed to swell—her breath was labored—she couldn't embrace him tightly enough. She let her hands caress his neck as they kissed—let her fingers run through his thick, soft hair. She wouldn't worry about work or the city or Monday. She'd have this gorgeous, masculine, fun, powerful man all to herself for as long as she could. She'd imagine she was worthy of him—that he found her as attractive as she found him. She'd be shoved back into reality soon enough. But for now she'd bathe in his embraces—soak in his kisses. And for now—she'd imagine that it would never end.

CHAPTER ELEVEN

Chatting with Patty as she stepped off the elevator had been nice. Even fighting the post-holiday, grouchy-driver traffic hadn't been too bad. But when Reese hadn't shown up for work by eleven that Monday morning, Breck had begun to feel quite insecure.

The drive back to the city from the Thatcher farm had been fine. Breck sensed Reese was having as much anxiety as she was about returning. Having to leave his mother standing on the farmhouse porch in tears hadn't helped matters. Still, when he'd dropped her off at her apartment Sunday night, he'd kissed her good bye—a long, passionate kiss, at that—and said he'd see her in the morning. Yet, here it was eleven a.m., and he was nowhere to be found.

In fact, it wasn't until after lunch that she received a message from him—on her voicemail. It seemed he'd be working out of town. Something he couldn't talk about requiring him to stay away for some time.

"I'll be gone until the fifteenth," his voice told her on the recorded phone message. "But don't worry, I'll call you."

Breck shook her head in disbelief. The fifteenth! That was two weeks! Certainly he'd had cases take him away for that long before, but things were different now. Weren't they? How would she endure? Already she'd been feeling very insecure about what had transpired between her and Reese at his parents' home over the holiday weekend.

Was it just a weekend fling? she wondered almost every moment throughout the day. Would he return and decide he'd made a mistake in getting involved with someone from work? She became so anxious she nearly threw up!

Even when the girls came over that night after work—Sherryl with chocolate-dipped strawberries—Kay with a new quilt square she'd been working on—Barb with her no-nonsense commands of "Buck up! He loves you"—even Trixie and her soothing manner—even with her best friends surrounding her, Breck felt hopeless, anxious.

Then, at about nine p.m. as Breck sat with her friends, trying to tell herself that all was well, the phone rang.

"Hello?" Breck answered, her voice quivering with hopeful anticipation.

"Breck?" It was Reese. Breck sighed and let a tear escape and travel down one cheek.

"Reese!" She couldn't stop the frantic sound in her voice. "H-how are you?" she stammered.

"Terrible," he grumbled. "I'm here, and you're

there." She smiled, and a small wave of relief broke over her.

"Is everything okay?" she asked. "When you didn't come into work this morning…I was really worried." It was hard to concentrate with four other women nodding and mouthing questions to her.

"I know, I'm sorry. I was going to call you last night before I left, but it was so late," he explained. "Hey, I can't talk long…but everything is fine. Okay?"

She wanted to shout to him, *But everything is not fine! I need reassurance. I need you!* Instead she managed, "Okay."

He must've heard the anxiety in her voice. "Breck…I really do have to go now," he told her. "But I mean it. Everything is fine. I don't want you to worry…about anything."

"Okay," she managed again.

"Hey…I'll tell you what," he began, "put in for a day off on the sixteenth. Tell personnel that I okayed it. I'll be back on the fifteenth, and the sixteenth we'll… do something. Okay?"

Breck felt mildly relieved, but she wondered if he was only trying to pacify her. Something was wrong.

"All right," she said. "Um…Reese?"

"Yeah?"

"Are you really okay?" she asked. There was a long pause, and it worried her.

"I am," is all he said.

"Well, I-I guess I'll see you on the sixteenth then," she mumbled.

"I'll call you in a couple of days," he told her. Then he added, "Breck, I have...I have to do this right now... before we go home for Christmas. And I know you're a worrier, so I don't want you to worry about anything while I'm gone. Everything is fine."

"All right, Reese," she managed. She felt better, for it sounded like he was still planning to take her back to the farm for Christmas. "I'll try not to."

"There's nothing to worry about. I promise," he told her. "I'll call you soon."

"Okay," she said, wiping the tears from her cheeks.

"And we'll make out...oops," he chuckled. "We'll make *up* for lost time when I get back."

Breck smiled. Maybe everything was going to be fine. "We will?" she asked.

"Oohhh, yeah!" he told her. "Good night, baby."

"Good night, Reese," she said. And he hung up.

"Well, I'm glad to see you've come around, Reese," Ben Thatcher told his son from his seat in his lounge chair by the fire. "It took a good many years...but it looks like you're finally over whatever sent you runnin' off."

Reese turned off his cell phone and sighed heavily. "Oh, I don't know if I'm over it, Pop. Just...just beyond it." He looked at the Christmas tree—his mother's beautiful Christmas tree—and thought how beautiful Breck had been when he'd dropped her off at her apartment before heading back to the farm.

"What did ol' Wilson say when you told him?" Ben Thatcher asked his son.

Reese chuckled. "He said, 'Good for you, Reese!' Though I know it puts him in a corner…trying to replace me."

"Oh, he'll find someone," Ben yawned. "A good investigator is easy to find. A good, hard-workin' man, however…ain't." Ben yawned again, this time adding a stretch for his back. "Still, I think you should've told your little treat there what you're up to."

Reese hung his head. He did feel guilty for not telling Breck that when he'd dropped her off the night before, realizing his mind and soul were whacked—that his life was messed up—he'd turned back around and headed for home. But he had a plan, and he needed time to implement a few things—get his head together before he faced her again.

"I know," Reese admitted. "But I think she'll understand someday."

"Oh, she will," Ben said. "She's a jewel. And you're a lucky man."

"I know," Reese said. "I just hope I can stay lucky."

❦

That night after the girls had gone—as she lay in bed attempting to find a way to get some sleep—Breck thought over the phone conversation she'd had with Reese.

"Stay calm," she told herself out loud. "Just stay calm."

If only he'd said, "I love you, Breck." If only he'd said, "I miss you," or something simple like, "I can't live without you." Then she'd be able to endure two weeks without him. But he hadn't said any of those things, and she was left to find a way to function for the next two weeks.

❦

Breck did function for the next two weeks. Perhaps not very efficiently, but she did function. She woke up, went to work, came home, and baked herself silly trying to stay busy. She tried to breathe and live—attempted to find ways of not worrying about Reese and what the future held or didn't hold for her where he was concerned. Still, it was more than merely difficult. For ever since returning from the Thatcher's farm—ever since Reese had kissed her and left her in her apartment that Sunday night over two weeks before—Breck had been unable to find a moment of happiness. Yes, he'd called her every few days, and each time he encouraged her—told her not to worry, that they'd spend time together when he returned. But it was hard. If only he'd give her more—a confession of sorts—of love. Of course, she hadn't told him she loved him—for what if he hadn't been ready to hear it? Then things might truly be ruined.

With each passing day, city life depressed Breck more and more. She was dissatisfied with it—angry with it—unsettled. Each time she'd think of Katie and Keith and their two adorable little girls—each time she'd think of Marjie and Ben and Nick and Bobby—each time she'd remember the sensations that ran through her body at being held in Reese's arms and kissed by him—every time she thought of the life she'd led for four days over the Thanksgiving holiday—she experienced despair.

Oh, she realized that everything about that weekend had been glamorized in a way. No one had worked from sunup to sundown trying to make a living off farming. No one had gotten hurt or hurt anyone. No one had worried about bills or making ends meet. She knew the weekend was rosy. Still, she also knew Reese belonged to that life. She'd seen it in him every moment they were there—the way he worked so physically hard helping his dad and brothers with chores, the contented smile on his face when he looked out to the pastures to see nothing but snow and cattle and sky. And she remembered the smile on his face when they'd stood inside the old farmhouse Thanksgiving night. Reese loved that house, and it loved him. Breck had felt it wash over her like a warm rain. She'd loved the house too, and the memory of it had helped her a bit over the past couple of weeks while Reese was out of town. If she felt tears of discouragement coming on, she'd take a moment or two and daydream—dreams of being married to Reese Thatcher and living in the old Thatcher farmhouse—dreams of rounding up cattle in the fall, calving in the spring, bringing in wheat and alfalfa in the summer—and dreams of walking through the woods near the old farmhouse, hunting for the perfect Christmas tree.

It was cruel, that's what it was, she often thought. Cruel to place such a man in her path if she couldn't have him. Cruel to show her such a wonderful life if she couldn't live it. Still, Reese had called her every few nights while he was gone, and tomorrow—tomorrow he would be back. Wouldn't he?

December fifteenth had been an excruciatingly terrible day for Breck. So much had gone wrong at work. The Allen case was getting very ugly; the Morgan and Dalton cases were worse. After work, Breck plopped down on the sofa in her apartment with a spoon in her mouth, a jar of peanut butter in one hand, and a package of milk chocolate chips in the other. On days like this, Breck wondered if she could keep going. Especially now that the part of her job she'd always enjoyed was absent— that being Reese. She choked back the tears that welled up in her eyes at the thought of him. She was hanging on for tomorrow—maybe by the skin of her teeth, but she was hanging on. Tomorrow Reese would be back, and she would know: had he changed his mind about her or not?

There was a knock on the door, and with a heavy sigh, Breck set down the peanut butter and chocolate chips, but not before filling her mouth with one last delicious blob of the two combined. Therefore, when she opened the door to see Reese standing before her, for once her mouth didn't drop open in astonishment— it couldn't! It was glued shut with peanut butter.

"Hi," he said, smiling rather apologetically at her.

"Hi," Breck managed after finally choking down the stuff in her mouth. It was an awkward moment, and uncertainty hung heavy in the air.

"You wanna grab a coat and come out with me for a little while?" Reese asked. Breck felt anxiety and joy at the same time, and it was rather uncomfortable.

"Work go okay today?" he asked once they were in his pickup. Breck swallowed hard. He was making small talk. Not a good sign. Her insides began to quiver with apprehension. Was he taking her out to break off everything with her?

"It was ugly," came her honest answer.

He smiled. "I can imagine," he said.

"How was your trip?" Breck couldn't help but ask.

"Very productive and enlightening," he answered.

"Oh, that's nice," she said.

A few minutes later, Reese parked the pickup in an empty field just outside of the city limits. Breck was afraid to look at him. What would she see—guilt, regret—pity?

"Come on," Reese said, stepping out of the pickup. Breck opened her door and slowly stepped out too. "Come here," he said, and she watched, puzzled as he took an old quilt from behind the pickup seat and spread it over the hood of the pickup. She was startled when he suddenly took hold of her waist, lifting her up and setting her on the hood. He climbed on beside her, stretched out on his back, tucked his hands behind his head, and sighed, "Ahhhhhh."

Breck was completely confused.

"Look at those stars," Reese mumbled. Breck looked up to see the clear night sky sparkling with bright starlight. "You can't see them from the city. You have to get out here away from the lights to see them."

If he were getting ready to let her down easy—throw a fish back in the lake—this seemed a strange way to do it. Breck braced herself. It had been wonderful, her weekend romance with her boss. It had been fantastic actually, and she would remember it forever. That's what she kept telling herself—better to have loved and lost, as the old cliché went. Yet she could feel the hard lump developing in her throat—the nausea rising in her stomach.

"Wait until we get back out to the farm," he said. "Remember how amazing stars are out there? I'd forgotten how amazing they were until we were there for Thanksgiving."

"You mean…you still want me to go there for Christmas?" Breck asked. She couldn't help it! Her heart was hammering so fast she thought it might knock her off the pickup altogether.

Reese frowned and looked over at her. "Of course," he said. "You haven't changed your mind, have you?" The expression on his face was truly that of panic.

Breck smiled, relief beginning to find its way into her body. "No. No, of course not."

"Whew!" Reese sighed, shaking his head. "You scared me. I thought you'd gone off and found yourself a better man while I was gone."

Breck breathed a sigh of relief. *Men are so clueless*, she thought. Accidentally then, she spoke her thoughts out loud.

"Like I'd ever find a better man than you," she mumbled. She blushed when she heard Reese chuckle.

"You didn't worry too much while I was gone, did you, Breck?" he asked her, sitting up and taking her chin in one hand.

Breck gazed into his eyes. They were so beautiful; *he* was so beautiful.

"I want you to tell me the truth…because…I've been a little wrapped up in getting myself straightened out these past couple of weeks, and…and I want to make sure that you didn't worry too much…you know…doubt me…my feelings for you," he said.

The moment had come, and Breck knew it. Oh, everything had been perfect over Thanksgiving—the place, the man, the flirting, the romance, the kissing. But life wasn't perfect, and if she hoped to really have Reese in her life forever, she needed to confide in him— be honest with him—let him know her true feelings.

"I-I did worry," she confessed. "I thought you…I thought you had changed your mind and decided that Thanksgiving was nice but reality was back now."

He closed his eyes for a moment and exhaled a guilty sigh. "I'm sorry, Breck. I-I was kind of messed up after Thanksgiving. Not about you…about me. I had to get some things straight in my mind, and to be honest, I had to be where I couldn't get my hands on you in order to think straight. Do you understand?"'

"Of course not," she said, smiling at him. But she did understand—and she was flattered as well as encouraged.

"I'm sorry," he said again. "But I'm cool now. I know what I need to do, where I need to be, and... and who I need to be with," he said, reaching over and taking her chin in his hand.

Suddenly then, he pushed her down so she was lying on the hood of the truck, reached over her, and pulled the quilt up, wrapping them in it.

"I wasn't just messing around over Thanksgiving, Breck," he told her as he hovered over her—his mouth a mere breath from her own. "But you sure did a number on me."

"Really?" she couldn't help asking. For she still needed reassurance. The past two weeks had been a miserable mess of worry, doubt, and loneliness.

"Oh, yeah," he said, grinning at her. Breck sighed as she felt him kiss her upper lip gently. "Come on, Breck," he whispered, kissing her lower lip once. "Throw me for another loop." He kissed her lower lip again. "I promise, I'll land on my feet this time."

And with that Reese's lips blended with Breck's in a kiss of reassurance—at first. Reassurance quickly gave way to desire and passion—affirmation—and Breck knew then that whatever the future may bring to her where Reese Thatcher was concerned, his attention to her, his affections, had been and were sincere. No, he hadn't professed love to her. But she hadn't professed it to him either. Maybe he was as frightened to confess it as she was. Maybe he just liked her an awful lot. But *like* could eventually grow into love. Couldn't it? She knew it could. And so she reveled in the moment—

in the feel of being wrapped in his arms under a sky full of stars. Reveled in his kiss and the knowledge that she "did a number" on him. And besides, Christmas was coming! Perhaps Christmas would be as magical as Thanksgiving had been. Perhaps come Christmas morning, she would find Reese Thatcher waiting for her under the tree. Oh, what a gift that would be!

CHAPTER TWELVE

"Breck, can I see you in my office for a minute?" Reese asked as he walked by her desk after lunch. Tomorrow—they were leaving for Christmas with his family tomorrow! Breck could hardly wait! The days since Reese's return from being out of town had been wonderful. He'd come over to her apartment every night, and they'd talked or watched movies—laughed and kissed. Breck was feeling much more confident of the sincerity of Reese's feelings for her. And now—now work was almost over for more than a week, and they would be back at the farm by tomorrow night!

"Yes," Breck answered. "I'll be right there." Reese had been working like a plow horse trying to get some loose ends tied up before leaving for Christmas. Breck couldn't believe how much time he was putting in at the office. In fact, she'd been amazed he'd even taken lunch that day.

Stepping into his office, she obeyed when he said, "Close the door, will you?" Once the door was closed, she gasped, dropping the yellow legal pad and pen she'd been holding in her hand as Reese took her shoulders, pushing her back against the door before smothering her in a hard, driven kiss. Breck wrapped her arms around his neck—instantly lost in the depth of their kiss. He was like a hungry lion—kissing her with a sort of ravenous appetite, a barely restrained desire! Oh, how she loved the feel of being kissed by him—the way his powerful hands traveled over her arms, resting at her waist a moment—his fingers pressing the small of her back, his thumbs briefly tracing the curve of her ribs. She sighed when he gathered her in his arms at last—gathered her in his arms and against the strength of his warm, strong body. Anyone would've thought he hadn't kissed her for a month rather than a mere sixteen hours.

After several minutes, his mouth left hers, and he smiled down at her, still holding her against the door. "Just needed a little dessert after lunch," he chuckled.

"Oh my heck!" Breck exclaimed with a smile. She was again amazed at his ability to keep her blushing.

"Now, you get back to work," he told her. "Quit trying to distract me. I have a lot to do before I can leave tomorrow." She shook her head and gasped when he swatted her on the rear end as she opened his office door.

"Reese!" she scolded in a whisper, looking up at the angle of the security camera above her desk and hoping it hadn't caught anything on tape. Still, she smiled at him—delighted—for, although her mother would've had a fit at his spanking her like that, she'd seen Reese's father do the same thing to his mother at least twice a day over Thanksgiving—and she liked the idea Reese would think of doing the same to her.

Still, it was hard to concentrate on anything after being ravaged in his office. Breck was even more distracted—fumbling papers, dropping pens. But the end of the day did come, and somehow, Breck felt as if work would never be the same again. It had been very different when she'd returned from her last visit out to the farm. But now—now she sensed it would be even more so on her return from this one. A small flicker of worry began to spark in the back of her mind because she knew Reese belonged away from the city, out in the open, working hard. But this trip back—what if he began to know it too? What if he decided to stay?

Breck shook her head, trying to dispel her worries. It was going to be wonderful—Christmas with Reese's family. And she was going to enjoy it.

"Oh, you're here, you're here, you're here!" Marjie Thatcher greeted, wiping the flour from her hands onto her apron and throwing her arms around Breck's neck. The house felt and smelled like heaven—warm, friendly, the scents of pine and gingerbread heavy in the air. "We thought you'd never get here," Marjie explained. "Were the roads pretty bad, Reese?"

The roads had been bad. A big snowstorm had begun dumping snow about an hour from the farm, and it made for a stressful drive.

"There're roads out there?" Reese teased. He smiled and embraced his mother. "The last twenty miles were really bad. I stopped and chained up, though. And we're fine." Marjie stood on her toes and kissed her son's cheek.

"Well, you're here now, and, Breck, we've got gingerbread men going in the kitchen. Do you wanna help?" Marjie asked.

Breck couldn't help smiling. It felt like—like *she'd* come home—not just that Reese had.

"Of course!" Breck giggled.

"Not before I get my hug," Ben said, approaching then. Breck smiled as he wrapped her in his strong arms and kissed her cheeks. "Welcome back, sugar," he added.

"Thank you for having me," she told him. Reese helped Breck take off her coat, hanging it on the coatrack behind the door.

"Better get in the kitchen. Mom will have my hide if I mess up her gingerbread men," Reese chuckled, kissing Breck quickly on the cheek. Yes, they'd have to share one another now—with Reese's family. But somehow, Breck didn't mind too awfully much.

"Hey, Breck," Nick greeted as Breck followed Marjie into the kitchen.

"Hi," Breck responded with a smile.

"Man! Reese hasn't been home this much in years!" Bobby told her. Breck was curious when Nick jabbed Bobby in the ribs with one elbow.

"You've eaten the heads off again?" Marjie exclaimed. "You boys…get out! Out! Get in there and mess up your daddy's project!"

"Daddy never has projects, Mom," Bobby said. "Besides, yours taste better." Picking up another gingerbread man off the cooling rack, Bobby bit off its head and smiled when his mother spanked him as he left the room.

Nick followed his brother out, and Marjie said, "Look at that! They always do this. Every year when I'm making my gingerbread men, they sneak in here when my back is turned and bite the heads of at least a dozen!"

Breck couldn't help smiling at the sad remains of a dozen headless gingerbread men.

Her smile broadened as she watched Marjie begin popping the remains in her mouth, saying, "Still, it gives me an excuse to taste my own baking." Holding out a half-eaten gingerbread man to Breck, she added, "Try one. See what you think."

Eat a cookie after Nick or Bobby had already bitten it? Normally the idea would've churned Breck's stomach. But there was something about Reese's family—something clean and safe. So she took the cookie offered to her and ate it.

"Mmmm!" she mumbled. "Mrs. Thatcher! This is delicious!" Breck enjoyed the smile of pride that spread across Marjie's face.

"Thanks. I think they're pretty good myself," Marjie said.

Marjie helped Breck tie a red apron on, handed her a blob of gingerbread dough and a rolling pin, and asked, "So…how has work been?"

Breck looked quickly to her. Her question had sounded like she already knew the answer. "Okay. We have some nasty cases in right now…and they kind of wear on me."

"I can imagine," Marjie said. "Do you…do you think you'll work there for long?"

Breck shrugged. "I don't know. It does pay well. But…"

"Money isn't everything," Marjie stated.

"That's for sure," Breck agreed.

"Has Reese been behaving himself? Where you're concerned, I mean?"

Breck blushed slightly. How embarrassing to have your boyfriend's mother asking such a question. And after all, she did consider Reese to be her boyfriend.

"Of course," Breck assured her.

Marjie sighed with relief. "I'm sure it's hard for him…but he's a good boy." Marjie smiled and popped a pinch of dough into her mouth. "Katie and the girls will be by later," she said. "Can you believe tomorrow is Christmas Eve? Whew! It sure snuck up on me this year."

"I-I brought a few things for everyone, Mrs. Thatcher," Breck told her then. "Would it be okay if I put them under your tree? I noticed you've got quite a pile going already."

Breck adored the way Marjie's eyes lit up at the mention of gifts. "Of course, sweet pea! But…you really didn't need to bring anything."

"I wanted to. You all have been so kind to me…

letting me impose on both of your major holidays and..." Breck began. She paused, however, when she felt Marjie place one hand over her own.

"You are not imposing, sugar," Marjie said, looking Breck squarely in the eyes. "You're...like one of the family." Breck felt a sweet, honeyed warmth drizzle over her. This woman was an angel, and Christmas was going to be wonderful.

As usual, Breck found herself lying awake by four a.m. Christmas Eve morning. All her life she'd loved Christmas Eve even more than Christmas Day! Christmas Eve seemed to hold a certain wonder and magic for her that somehow vanished an hour or so after rising on Christmas morning. She knew Reese's mother left the lights on her tree burning all night, and she figured they'd be beautiful in the darkness of early morning.

Quietly, she dressed and tiptoed out into the hallway. Even in the hallway she could see the colorful shadows on the walls of the front room beyond, assuring her the tree was indeed aglow. Stepping into the front room, she sighed with delight at the sight of the tree. Someone had been up before her too, for there was a fire blazing in the fireplace.

Breck startled as she sat down on the sofa when she heard Ben say, "I like a woman who can get out of bed in the morning." Breck turned around to see Ben lounging in his favorite chair. No doubt he'd been out already. Probably the boys had been too—feeding the stock and making sure the ice in the watering tanks was busted up.

"I'm sorry," Breck told him. "Am I disturbing you?"

Ben chuckled. "Me? No," he assured her. "Reese, however…now that's a different story, isn't it?" Breck blushed. "I like the way you got him thinkin', Breck. He needed to do some hard of it."

"I'm sure I didn't have anything to do—" Breck began.

"Oh, I'm sure you did," Ben interrupted. "His mother and I have been poundin' our heads against the wall for years now." The man sighed and shook his head. "That deal with Tommy…it just cut him so deep. I don't think we realized how angry and hurt he was at the time. But it wasn't long before we realized he'd suffered some severe damage emotionally."

Breck didn't say a word. She wanted nothing more at that moment than to hear what Reese's father had to say.

"I think he felt guilty at first," he continued, "I think he felt bad that Tom died and he didn't. Then it turned into fear…a realization that a man can die. Boys…they have this misconception of being immortal, you see. When they're young they think they're so tough that nothin' can touch them. It's a hard thing to see your first friend die…and it sure hit Reese the wrong way.

"After the guilt left and the fear set in, anger was next. He was infuriated that the sheriff couldn't give him an answer….about what had happened to Tom. He ranted and raved and swore for weeks about it.

Rage turned to blame…blaming farm life and small-town mentality for the accident and for not finding an answer. He decided then that he could single-handedly save the world." Ben smiled at Breck and added, "Personally, I think he read one too many superhero comic books as a kid."

Breck giggled.

"So for years we've been watchin' him struggle, tryin' to find himself, where he should be and the like," Ben said with a sigh. Then he smiled at Breck. "Then you come along, and he finally seems to be pullin' his head out of the bucket."

"I'm sure it's not me," Breck told him. And she was sure. "Maybe…maybe just coming home at Thanksgiving—"

"He wasn't plannin' on comin' home for Thanksgiving…'til you came along," Ben explained. "Ahh…but I'm interruptin' your peace and quiet here," he said, pulling the handle at the side of his chair and sitting upright.

"Oh, no!" Breck argued. "I love talking with you! It's the first chance we've had to talk, really."

Ben chuckled, rather swaggering over to her and cupping her cheek in one strong, roughened hand. "We'll find our time, pretty girl. Don't you worry." And with that, he left Breck alone with the fire and the tree and the feelings of happiness and comfort.

As day broke, everyone else in the Thatcher family trickled into the front room and kitchen. Breck could feel the excitement in the air. Everyone was excited about Christmas Eve, including the men. Katie and her family arrived just after breakfast, and Breck giggled as she watched Lizzy and Sarah shaking the gifts she'd set under the tree for them the night before. She hoped that the stuffed cat with her stuffed litter of kittens would soothe some of the child's disappointment at Breck being unable to produce a living litter for her. She smiled at the memory of Lizzy asking her if she'd have some babies for her Uncle Reese. It *had* been a funny moment.

Most of the late morning and early afternoon, Breck accompanied Marjie as she delivered various baskets filled with breads, cookies, nuts, meats, and cheeses to family friends of surrounding farms. It was wonderful. Reese had volunteered to drive his mother on her errands—being that the storm the night before had left driving a bit dangerous—and it was wonderful, sitting next to Reese in his pickup as his mother chattered away excitedly. It seemed she told Breck the entire family history of every family she visited, and Breck giggled at her merry mood.

Christmas Eve dinner at the Thatcher farm proved very traditional, with ham, potatoes, and all the fixings. Breck nearly burst into tears as she watched Ben coax his granddaughters up onto his lap as he sat in his lounge chair and began reading from the book of Luke—the story of the birth of the Christ child. The tree twinkled, the fire burned, and Reese, his brothers,

Katie and Keith, and Marjie sat in awed quiet as Ben read to the girls.

After the bible story, Marjie handed Ben a large, beautifully illustrated copy of *The Night Before Christmas*. Breck watched as Lizzy's and Sarah's eyes widened with excitement at the prospect of catching Santa leaving presents under their own tree.

All during Ben's reading the stories, Breck had been bathing in the warmth and power of Reese's embrace as he held her. But he rose suddenly, excusing himself to do a couple of chores outside.

"Do you want me to help?" Breck asked.

Reese smiled at her. "Not just now. You stay inside where it's warm."

Instantly, Nick plopped down next to Breck on the sofa. Bobby followed shortly, sitting on the other side of her.

"Don't worry, Reese," Nick chuckled. "We'll keep her warm for you."

"You boys behave," Marjie scolded, giggling at the same time.

"I'll be back in a minute," Reese assured Breck.

And so she settled back down and watched Lizzy and Sarah hop down off their grandpa's lap when the story was through and go back to investigating the presents under the tree.

Everyone was talking about Christmases past— laughing and telling stories.

"Remember that dog-ugly tree Pop brought home the year mom had her surgery?" Bobby asked.

"How could we forget?" Katie sighed as everyone else laughed.

"It looked like a big twig with a few pine needles on it," Nick told Breck.

"That there was a good tree," Ben defended himself. "It looked just fine when I first chopped it down."

"But then you rolled your pickup with the tree in the back...and by the time he got home...it was a twig with a few pine needles," Nick laughed.

"It was a lovely tree, Ben," Marjie assured her husband. She smiled at him, and he winked at her.

Reese returned then, brushing the snow off the sleeves of his coat.

"Hey, Breck," he said, "you wanna grab your coat? I've got something to show you."

"Sure," Breck said. She was excited about the prospect of spending some time alone with Reese. She didn't care if she froze to death riding on the back of the four-wheeler while they traveled around breaking up ice in water tanks. She just wanted some time alone with the man—with the man she loved.

Reese helped Breck put her coat on, and she frowned, puzzled as the entire family rose from their seats and followed them to the front door. And when Reese opened the front door to reveal an old sleigh—adorned with jingle bells and hitched to a strong-looking mare—she gasped, and everyone smiled at her.

"Wanna go for a ride?" Reese asked her.

Breck smiled at him, her eyes filling with tears of joy. "Of course!" she told him.

He helped her into the sleigh, tucked an old quilt tightly over her lap, and climbed in next to her. As he snapped the reins lightly on the horse's back, the sleigh lurched forward, and everyone stood on the front porch waving. It wasn't long before the horse was trotting along at a steady pace—the bells jingling, matching its rhythm.

"It's a 'one-horse open sleigh,'" Reese pointed out.

"I got that," Breck giggled, wrapping her arms tightly around one of his strong ones.

They rode in silence for quite a while, for it seemed that neither one of them wanted to talk and ruin the music of the bells and the sleigh sliding along in the snow. Frost fell through the air, sifting onto the surface of the snow-covered ground like a billion tiny diamonds. The stars were twinkling overhead—bright, happy, and beautiful. It was a moment borne of dreams.

"You're quite the romancer," Breck said quietly.

Reese smiled. "I try," he told her.

Some time later, Breck looked ahead of them and recognized the silhouette of the old Thatcher farmhouse on the dark horizon. Only—this time—something was different. As they turned toward the front of the house, Breck gasped when she saw the beautiful twinkles of color dotting the snow on the ground in front of the house. A brightly lit Christmas tree stood in the bay window at the front of the house, shining out like a beacon of heaven.

"Reese!" she gasped and heard him chuckle.

"Do you like it?" he asked her, pulling the horse to a stop in front of the house.

Breck shook her head and let one tear escape each eye. "It's...it's too beautiful for words!" she whispered.

Reese smiled and climbed down from the sleigh. "Come on then. I have something to show you."

Breck stumbled once as he helped her out of the sleigh, for she couldn't take her eyes off the tree in the window. It seemed to illuminate the entire outside of the house as well. She could've sworn the paint looked fresher.

"Now...stand right here," Reese instructed, positioning her in a spot in the front yard directly in front of the house. "Don't move, okay?"

"Okay," she agreed. She continued to stare at the beautiful tree—at the happy-looking house. It was amazing what a Christmas tree did for a house: it made it a home.

Reese dashed up the front porch stairs and hunkered down for a moment. And then, suddenly, the outside of the house lit up as cascades of tiny white icicle lights glimmered from every eave and trim.

Breck gasped again—breathless for a moment as she took in the wonder of the lights. Reese jogged down the porch steps and came to stand next to her, inspecting the wonder himself.

"Pretty nice, if I do say so myself," he said.

Breck looked at him. "Y-you did all this?" she asked.

"Yeah," he said, pulling her into his arms. "I about broke my dang neck too."

Breck returned his embrace, smiling up into his handsome face. "I'm glad you didn't."

"Me too," he whispered before kissing her upper lip lightly. Breck felt the butterflies take flight in her stomach as his kiss lingered on her lower lip then. He'd kiss her lower lip twice before really kissing—she knew it. He often started their kisses in the same teasing manner. It was as if he were preparing her for greater things to come. And greater things always did.

They stood there in the snow in front of the old farmhouse—lost in their warm, moist kisses as the frost sifted down over them.

All at once, Reese pushed her away from him and, grinning at her, said, "Come on. There's more."

Breck giggled, delighted as he pulled her up the front porch steps and into the house. Once he'd closed the door behind them, Breck looked up and drew in a quick breath as she saw the fresh beauty of the room.

"Reese," she breathed. It was incredible. The lights from the tree cast color on the freshly painted, white walls. A fire burned warm in the fireplace, and the floor had been polished.

"It still smells like paint...but it looks good, huh," he told her, tugging on her hand, coaxing her further into the room.

"It looks perfect," Breck whispered. And it did!

Reese clapped his gloved hands together and nodded with pride. "I worked hard to get it this way."

Breck frowned and looked up to him. "*You* worked hard?"

"Yep," he told her. "I know you assumed I was working a case while I was gone, Breck," he confessed. "But I was here...working on the house...and working some things out in my mind. Are you mad?"

There was a part of her that was angry. He'd been here on the farm enjoying his family and the escape from the city, while she'd been worried and miserable in the city? And yet, it was *his* family—his family's farm. She had no right to be angry, and suddenly—she wasn't. Fear, however, began to creep into her mind and heart. Reese had obviously put a lot of time and effort into fixing up this old house. Why? Was he thinking of returning? Would he leave her in the city and...

"I quit," he said, his smile fading.

"What?" Breck asked. Her heart began to hammer hard in her chest—an anxious, frightened kind of hammer.

Reese nodded. "That night we got home from Thanksgiving...I dropped you off, turned around to drive through the city back to my own house, and... and never made it. I came back here and spent some time talking with my parents. Then I worked on this house...worked hard physically, you know? I've missed that."

"What do you mean?" Breck asked. He'd quit? If he'd quit his job at Wilson Investigation, then Breck could only guess what was coming next—or at least part of what was coming next.

"I own this house, Breck," he told her. "I bought it

from Mom and Pop a few years back…the house and about two thousand acres."

"You're moving back?" she ventured. She felt light-headed—sick to her stomach. He was leaving the city—he was leaving her!

"You don't think I should?" He seemed concerned—seemed to doubt his decision—and Breck knew she must encourage him, for it was where he belonged, where he would be happy. And she wanted him to be happy.

"Oh, no," she stammered. "I…I think…I think it's wonderful."

Reese grinned then, his eyes narrowing as he searched her face. "Hold on a second," he told her. Then he walked to one corner of the room, lifted the lid on an old record player, and next—next Breck heard the melody of one of her favorite old Bing Crosby Christmas songs begin to play. Instantly, tears began to roll down her cheeks. It was a beautiful moment. The most beautiful, most heartbreaking moment she'd ever known. Reese was so excited about his decision to come home—wanted her to be excited for him. He'd gone to the trouble of finding her one of her favorite Bing Crosby songs, and all she could do was cry because she was devastated.

"Dance with me?" he asked, taking one of her hands in his. Breck wiped the tears from her cheeks and tried to smile.

As he led her in an old-fashioned waltz, he asked, "What's the matter, baby? Don't you like the house?"

"I love the house," she sniffled.

"Well, guess what, Miss Breck McCall?" he said, lowering his voice and stopping their waltz. Taking her face in his hands, he gazed down into her face and said, "I love *you*."

Breck closed her eyes for a moment, letting more tears escape down her cheeks. He'd said it! At last he'd said he loved her. But it was almost bittersweet. A long-distance relationship? Still, she loved him, and she didn't want to lose him.

"I love you too, Reese," she whispered, opening her eyes and looking up at him. "And I want you to be happy...here. You belong here."

"Do I?" he whispered, taking one of her hands in his, raising it to his lips, and kissing it tenderly.

"You do," she managed.

Breck gasped then, her tears turning to tiny rivulets as they streamed down her face—for Reese raised his other hand then—his fisted other hand. He opened it a moment later to reveal a beautiful diamond solitaire ring lying in his palm.

"You're all I want for Christmas," he said. "Every Christmas," he added, pushing the ring onto her appropriate finger. "Will you marry me, Breck? Will you quit your job in the city, give up everything you've worked so hard to achieve there...and be a farmer's wife?"

Breck buried her face in her hands and sobbed. This couldn't be happening! She shook her head, trying to dispel the dream—but it stayed. Reese stood there—

wiping the tears from her cheeks, kissing her forehead, and chuckling. It was real!

"Will you, Breck?" he asked again.

With rivers of tears rolling down her cheeks, Breck nodded and said, "Of course, I will!"

Instantly, she was in his arms, his mouth taking her own in a driven, passionate exchange. He was hers! Reese Thatcher would belong to her!

He released her, raised her hand to inspect the ring on her finger, and asked, "Do you like your Christmas present, baby?"

Suddenly, Breck gasped, horrified as she remembered something. "I only got you an electric razor!"

Reese laughed and pulled her into his arms again. "I love you, Breck McCall. And you found me…helped me remember who I was and what I love." He cupped her face in his hands and gazed down into her eyes. "Thank you."

Breck smiled and brushed the tears from her cheeks. "*You* are my dreams come true," she confessed.

Reese smiled, caressing her lips with his thumb. "Then I guess here…in this moment…in *our* house… all is right with the world. Isn't it?"

Breck nodded, and there in the old Thatcher family farmhouse, fragrant with the scent of a cedar fire and warm with the beauty and color of Christmas tree lights, Reese kissed her again—a long, adoring kiss that spoke of promised happiness and everlasting love.

EPILOGUE

It had been fun having the girls and their families out the day before. Breck couldn't believe how big Barb's, Kay's, Sherryl's, and Trixie's children were getting. But then again, her own children were growing up faster than she liked too. Breck shook her head, unable to believe for a moment that her daughter Bobbie was already five years old—and Scottie would be three next month! How time had flown since that first Christmas she and Reese had spent together—that first Christmas when he'd driven her out to their house on a horse-drawn sleigh and asked her to marry him.

Breck dusted the rest of the residual powdered sugar off the counter and into her hand. It was Christmas Eve day, and it had been wonderful! Breck had delivered baskets with Reese's mother in the morning and later watched Katie's girls show Bobbie and Scottie how to sprinkle powdered sugar over the gingerbread houses to look like snow. She giggled, thinking the children got more powdered sugar on themselves and the floor than they did the gingerbread houses.

And Reese would be home soon! How she missed

him every minute he was away from her. Anytime he was gone from the house doing chores or working with his father and brothers, she missed him. Their life together was wonderful! Oh, they worked hard and had their share of worries and challenges, but it was a life she'd once dreamed of—and her dreams had all come true. The new baby due in June would only add to Reese's joy and hers, and Breck knew that, come what may, the love she and Reese shared was deeper and stronger than most, and she was thankful for it.

She heard the kitchen door close and looked up to see her handsome husband brushing the snow from his coat sleeves. He stomped his work boots on the mat several times to free them of as much slush as possible before pulling them off and setting them aside. He took off his coat, hat, and gloves and laid them on the counter by the door.

"Hey, baby," he said, taking Breck in his arms and kissing her hard on the mouth. "Kids in bed?"

"Just now. They're waiting for you to tuck them in," Breck told him. "Brrr! Your cheeks are cold!"

"It's cold out there tonight," he explained. "But the sky is clear. Santa won't have any trouble finding our house," he chuckled.

"Well, I hope not," Breck giggled, "'cause Santa still has to assemble that dollhouse he's bringing for Bobbie."

"I'll run up and tuck them in." Reese smiled and kissed her cheek again. "Meet me in the front room in three minutes," he whispered. With a wink and a mischievous grin, he added, "I wanna make good use of that mistletoe you hung up in there."

He quickly kissed her cheek, and Breck giggled as she watched him saunter across the room in his stocking feet, bounding up the back stairs toward the kids' bedrooms.

Sighing with the pure contentment borne of love and Christmas Eve, she went into the front room, sat down on the sofa, and watched the lights of the Christmas tree twinkling in the bay window. Bing was crooning softly on the stereo. It was one of those rare moments a woman experiences when her mind, body, and soul find complete tranquility. She closed her eyes for a moment and breathed in the scent of their home—the warm aroma of fresh-baked cookies—of a cedar fire—of love.

"Merry Christmas, Mrs. Thatcher," Reese said. He took her hand, pulled her to her feet, and wrapped her in his arms.

"Merry Christmas, Mr. Thatcher," Breck whispered as he kissed her upper lip softly. He gently kissed her lower lip once—then a second time—and Breck's heart began hammering inside her chest as wildly as ever it did when Reese kissed her. His mouth captured hers for a moment, and she sighed—bathed in the warmth of love and desire.

Reese abruptly broke the seal of their kiss, distracted by the familiar squeak of the seventh step on the staircase.

"Kids? Get back to bed," Reese growled, in his most fatherly voice.

Breck smiled as she heard Bobbie's and Scottie's playful giggling as they scampered up the stairs and back to bed.

"They'll never get to sleep," Reese chuckled. "We'll be building that dollhouse 'til four in the morning."

Breck nodded and ran her fingers through her husband's hair. He needed a haircut. She let her fingers trace the outline of his mustache and goatee and then raised herself on the tips of her toes and kissed him softly on the mouth.

"Thank you for making all my dreams come true, Mr. Thatcher," she whispered.

"I love you, Mrs. Thatcher," he told her, tracing the curve of her face with the back of his hand.

"I love you too," she said, kissing him once more.

Again they were interrupted by one of the squeaky stairs, and Reese chuckled as they looked up to see their two little black-haired, freckle-faced babies, peering down at them through the wooden banister rails.

"We can't sleep, Daddy," Bobbie whined.

"Wead us a stowy, Daddy," Scottie begged. "Pwease?"

Breck smiled as her husband sighed. She knew he was tired. He'd worked hard all day getting everything finished so he would have minimal work the next. Still, she knew how the children tugged at his heartstrings.

"Okay," Reese agreed. "But you have to be in bed

before I get up the stairs," he said, releasing Breck and sprinting for the staircase.

Bobbie and Scottie erupted into giggles, fleeing up the stairs and down the hall to their bedrooms. Breck could hear their delighted laughter as Reese tickled and teased them before finally settling them for his own rendition of *The Night Before Christmas*.

Breck glanced to the beautiful Christmas tree standing in her bay window. She watched its lights for a moment—admired its beauty. Her life was more wonderful than she'd ever dreamed it could be. There were still good people and good things in the world. There was still true love—the unsurpassed kind—the kind she shared with Reese.

"Mommy!" she heard Scottie call. "Come hear the stowy wiff us."

Smiling, Breck climbed the stairs of the old Thatcher farmhouse to where her husband and children sat waiting to cover her face with kisses, warm her with their hugs, and keep her heart forever safe—enfolded in their love.

AUTHOR'S NOTE

Do you know what the funny thing is? When I first wrote *An Old-Fashioned Romance*, I thought everyone would hate it! I was so scared that my first contemporary story wouldn't be well-received that I included an Author's Note at the beginning of the book. It read thus:

An Old-Fashioned Romance is different than most of my other stories. First of all, it takes place in the here and now, rather than the past. It is also a mirrored reflection of many things and people I cherish.

In truth, I've been very unsettled about releasing this story…afraid it reveals too much about myself or that it doesn't have enough adventure to entertain the reader. However, those who have read it adore it—and it seems to strum a chord in their hearts…a tender chord often overlooked.

Therefore, I entrust it to you now, hoping you will enjoy reading it as much as I enjoyed pouring my heart into it.

To all of us…
And those 'Old-Fashioned' everythings we miss.

As the little "Author's Warning Label" read, I was afraid that sharing so much of my personal self might provide a target for hurt and harm—not only to my own heart and feelings but for loved ones making an appearance in the book as the fictional characters Barb,

Kay, Sherryl, and Trixie. However, *An Old-Fashioned Romance* didn't crash and burn. In fact, it is often listed as a reader favorite—and I'm so glad!

Therefore, having been inundated with requests for details about the inspiration for the book, I'm delighted to have this opportunity to add a little something to it for you—to once again give the reader a little insight into the workings of my mind and the beloved things of my heart that helped inspire this book.

Let's begin with pumpkins. Ah! Wonderful pumpkins! Oh, how I *love* pumpkins! Few things make my heart soar the way the vision of a field of pumpkins does. Yes, I've seen fields of tulips—acres upon acres of tulips blooming in fields that stretch off into the horizon nearly as far as the eye can see. I've see the waves of the sea rolling in—lapping or crashing upon the sand or rocks of the shore. I've seen snowy mountains—majestic in their white cloaks of winter beauty. Yet none of these thrill me the way a field of pumpkins does. I love them! I love the fascinating squash, so resplendent in orange, so perfect for making pie and jack-o'-lanterns, or for simply lingering on a front porch in glorious autumn. It's a happy thing, the pumpkin, and I love it! I write poetry about pumpkins, collect ceramic pumpkins for my kitchen, wear pumpkin-themed sweaters as often as I can September through November. I even had a pumpkin-themed guest room in my house in Colorado, and currently my office is blissful in pumpkin color and decor. In short, pumpkins make me happy! Just the sight of one (or a ton) lifts my soul to the very zenith of joy. Thus, in *An Old-Fashioned Romance*, Breck loves pumpkins too. Breck's adoration of the King of Squash is a not-so-secret reflection of my own pumpkin passion! (P.S. I *love* pumpkins!)

Pumpkin pie for breakfast on Thanksgiving morning? Of course! In the book, Reese's mom mentions that Reese's father likes to have pumpkin pie for breakfast on Thanksgiving morning. Well, who doesn't? My children can thank my kind, loving, understanding mother for that family tradition. Although we didn't have pumpkin pie for breakfast on Thanksgiving morning when I was growing up, we did have it for breakfast the following day. Once Kevin and I started our own family, pumpkin pie for breakfast became a tradition not only for Thanksgiving Day but also for two or three days following! I usually make ten or eleven pumpkin pies for Thanksgiving if we're having company for Thanksgiving dinner—a few less if we're not. That way there's always plenty of pumpkin pie for breakfast, lunch, and dinner! Breck's tried-and-true pumpkin pie recipe (included at the end of this Author's Note) is, in truth, my own recipe. Mmmm! I love pumpkin pie!

When I was six years old, my mom took me to a little craft evening with some ladies at church. There we were provided with old-fashioned wooden peg clothespins, red and blue paint, black yarn pom-poms, and some gold braid. Guess what we made? That's right—toy soldiers to hang on the Christmas tree! I remember making the toy soldiers—very vividly remember making them—and I remember hanging them on our Christmas tree every year after that. I love them! To me they were simply magical, and I cherished them because I remember Mom and me making them. When I left home, Mom gave me two of them, and my children hung them on our Christmas tree. Well, one year (being that I have three children and only had two toy soldiers) I sat down with my own children at our kitchen table, and we made some wooden peg toy soldiers of our own. Of course, my boys eventually began breaking up toothpicks, dipping them in red paint, and gluing them onto a few extra toy soldiers to make it look like they had been in battle. Needless to say, I felt the project needed to come to an end— and so did Reese's mom. I love those simple little clothespin soldiers my mom and I made when I was six. I wholeheartedly treasure them.

Some of my most tranquil moments have been spent in front of a Christmas tree, late at night, when all else is quiet and calm. In those moments I love to turn out all the lights (except for the ones on the tree, of course), put on a little *Christmas with Conniff* or *White Christmas* by Bing Crosby, and just sit in mesmerized wonder at the beauty of the Christmas tree and the season. Sometimes when I'm stressed—worried and feeling tired and perhaps discouraged—I can climb into bed, close my eyes, and envision those Christmas tree moments. Ahhh! I love the soothing, rather healing power of a Christmas tree.

Between 1992 and 1994, I met four women that would literally change my life—individuals that would become four pieces of my heart. Barbara, Dixie, Karen, and Sheri were and are absolute blessings from heaven—given to me to entertain, strengthen, support, and teach. The five of us met when we all lived in Rio Rancho, New Mexico, between 1992 and 1995—and such kindred spirits I could never have imagined. The laughter we've shared has nearly hospitalized us at times! The tears we've shed have kneaded our hearts near painfully. I really can't imagine my life without having been touched by these incredible friends.

The thing about the Groovy Chicks (as we came to be known) is that not only was our group relationship something to behold but my personal, individual relationships with each Groovy Chick is profound. Oddly, we came from about every different walk of life and had every different hobby or interest that you could imagine. Yet there's something—an invisible thread of commonality that glued us together. Barb, Kay, Trixie, and Sherryl are quite obviously based on my friends the Groovy Chicks.

As a collective group, you've never seen more waiters and waitresses have a better time serving customers or get bigger tips than those that served us anytime we were together. What fun we have with restaurant staffs! Furthermore, the one-liners that fly around the room anytime we're together could rival any favorite stand-up comic. To sum it up, when the Groovy Chicks convene, so does the entertainment.

Individually, each Groovy Chick has taught me, helped me, inspired me—been infused with my heart. I met Karen (Kay) first—a super sweet, book-reading quilter. Karen really does quilt and sew like the wind! Her house is always immaculate—very white and blue and homey—and she's a cookbook author. Karen's humor is borne of the fact that it is often unintentional—just something she says that comes out hilarious when she didn't necessarily mean it to be that way. She's the "sweet" chick, and we all adore her. Karen sprinkles serenity and smiley-faces in her wake. She's like a little pink petunia that makes you feel as if all is right with the world when you're with her. Karen—the book-reading, quilting, cookbook-authoring, seamstressing Groovy Chick.

Dixie is one of the three farm girls in the Groovy Chick contingency. I once heard her get onto one of her kids for chewing with his mouth open. "Close your mouth. We don't need to see you chewing your cud," she told him. If that doesn't reveal the farm girl in her, I don't know what would. Dixie makes the most delicious homemade bread and rolls—by hand! In fact, she had to have carpal tunnel surgery. The cause of her carpal tunnel—kneading so much bread dough! Dixie is also hilarious. Some of the things that shoot out of Dixie's mouth can leave the rest of us rolling on the floor with laughter at the moment and bursting into random giggles when remembering it years later. Furthermore, Dixie (like Trixie) really does sculpt her food! I have photos of pancake remains jigsaw-puzzled together to form North America, French fries stacked into a perfect little log cabin, and cake frosting literally sculpted into a bird. You never know what the remains of Dixie's meal are going to end up as—artistically speaking. Dixie—the patient, self-sacrificing, sultry-voiced, food artist Groovy Chick.

Now, Barbara—she's the adventurer of the group. A one-time "survival guide," Barbara could get you through anything! And she'd catch, cook, and feed you a rattlesnake while she did it. The camping, hiking, rattlesnake-cooker of the group, Barbara doesn't mince words. She's straightforward and matter-of-fact, and she has the most contagious laugh I've ever heard in my entire life! Just hearing Barbara burst into laughter can send you into your own peals of chortling—whether or not you even heard what made her laugh or thought it was funny yourself. She's also a classic one-liner artist. One of my favorites (which we all still quote): upon practicing a group song to be performed at an assisted living place and asked to sing alto, Barbara said, "You have to have a chest hair to sing that low!" I'm certain it's one of those *you had to be there to appreciate it things*, but I promise, it was hysterical! Barbara—the rattlesnake-cooking, one-liner dropping, "sheepishly jogging" (that's a long story), contagious-laugh laugher Groovy Chick.

And then there's Sheri. Oh my heck, Sheri! Sheri is not only the professional photographer of the group but the comedy relief! Sheri lightens my heavy heart and can add a glimmer of spark to my soul when things seem darkest. Sheri's my crazy-silly-fun friend! The adventures we've had where betta fish, tulip festivals, funny videos, and "The Twelve Days of Christmas" are concerned are literally indescribable. Sheri can grow anything; any plant loves her and thrives for her. She's an incredible photographer and *totally* would've captured the meeting of Breck and the Highwayman of Tanglewood with her camera. Most of all, she's hilarious! For example, she sent me a copy of the cover for my one of my books, *The Windswept Flame*, wherein she had computer-manipulated a photo of herself into the image to appear as if she were riding on the back of the horse with the silhouetted cowboy, changed the title to *The Windswept **Friend***, and inserted back cover text that titled another book as *Sheri and The Caballero*. Sheri—the photographing, green-thumbed, adventuring, comedic Groovy Chick.

My friendships with Barbara, Dixie, Karen, and Sheri have been absolutely life-changing! Each of these four friends has enriched my life in ways they probably will never know or understand. I'm thankful for them—know that I am blessed to have them—and I'm grateful for the inspiration they offered for this book.

An Old-Fashioned Romance Trivia Snippets

Snippet #1—Reese really did get his name because my favorite candy is miniature Reese's Peanut Butter Cups!

Snippet #2—In 1985 I babysat two little boys every

day for a time—brothers, ages five and three. Just after the youngest was born, the older brother asked his mom if she would have some kittens for him next!

Snippet #3—One of the Groovy Chicks had a real-life experience that inspired the rotten, hoochie character Jamie in *An Old-Fashioned Romance*.

Snippet #4—As a child, one of the Groovy Chicks actually experienced "finding the perfect angel costume in the back of her mother's closet"—which, of course, inspired the entire "sexy angel" thread in my book *Love Me*.

Snippet #5—One of the Groovy Chicks is an incredible grammarian and owns an awe-inspiring vocabulary! I first heard the word *monosyllabic* (used in this book) drop from her lips, and long ago she challenged me to use the word *emasculate* in a book—which I did, in *Indebted Deliverance*.

Snippet #6—One of the Groovy Chicks loves rain—thus, the inspiration for the "kissing in the rain" scene in *Sudden Storms*.

Snippet #7—Each of the Groovy Chicks has at least one Marcia Lynn McClure book dedicated to her. In each of those books, there are hidden, personal tributes to that particular Groovy Chick.

Snippet #8—In *Shackles of Honor* the swans that are ever-floating over the surface of the lake whenever Cassidy is there are representations of the Groovy Chicks, as are the four elderly widows in *The Touch of Sage*.

As usual, I've babbled on too long. But before I go, please allow me to thank you for wandering through *An Old-Fashioned Romance* with me. I'll leave you now to run off and whip up a pumpkin pie and enjoy it all over again!

~Marcia Lynn McClure

Breck's Pumpkin Pie

2 nine-inch (uncooked) pie crusts (already placed in a pie plate, edges fluted, and set aside)

3 eggs

1 large can (29 oz.) of pumpkin

1 cup sugar

½ cup brown sugar

1 teaspoon salt

5 teaspoons pumpkin pie spice

2 ¼ cups evaporated milk

4 tablespoons flour

Combine all ingredients, and pour into crust in pie plate. Place in oven, lightly covering with a sheet of aluminum foil. Bake at 425ºF for 15 minutes, and then reduce oven heat to 350ºF and cook for 60 to 75 minutes more—or until knife inserted into the center of pie comes out clean. Cool before serving with fresh whipped cream!

And now, enjoy chapter one of the first book in
The McCall Trilogy,
The Foundling
(also available as Desert Fire)
by Marcia Lynn McClure.

CHAPTER ONE

She felt something on her face. It was cool, soothing, moist. Her throat burned and constricted and when she tried to swallow, she couldn't.

"Ma'am?" She heard the voice, but it seemed so far away. "Ma'am?" It came again, closer this time. "Can you hear me, ma'am?" A man's voice, deep and stern.

She attempted to speak, but found it impossible. She tried to nod in response, but her head was pounding like a drum was pinned up inside it.

"Open your eyes if you can. Open 'em," the voice insisted.

She opened her eyes just a slit and quickly clenched them shut again as searing rays of sunlight burned through her. She sensed movement and the demanding voice came once more.

"Now...try again."

It was a voice not to be ignored. She tried to lift her hand to shade her face, but her own body would not obey her mind's command. She opened her eyes slightly and when the sun didn't blind her painfully again, she was able to open them completely. Everything was blurry for several seconds but she could make out a dark figure bending over her.

"Can you see?" the voice asked firmly.

She blinked several times clearing her vision slightly.

"Yes," she mouthed, though no sound escaped her blistered lips. A hand slipped beneath her head and lifted it.

"Here...keep still and let this stay on your tongue for a minute," the voice said, and she felt the first cool, life giving drops of water moisten her mouth. She couldn't move her tongue at first, but the second time the stranger offered the water from the canteen, she was able to swallow it.

After several mouthfuls of water she felt more alert and realized her face, arms and shoulders felt tight and hot.

"Now...what's your name, girl? And how'd ya' end up out here?" the man asked.

She could see clearly then and for the first time she looked up into the face that belonged to the voice.

"I don't know," she answered in a forced whisper.

The man let out a sigh, tipped his hat back on his head and looked around with an expression of both bewilderment and annoyance.

"You don't know how you ended up lyin' out in the middle of nowhere, with nothin' or no one with you?" he asked, still looking around.

"No," she whispered, feeling suddenly terrified at the realization.

The stranger stood up and pulled his hat down into place again.

"Well...I guess I'll just haul ya' on home and we'll think on it from there." He walked over to a nearby tree and untied a horse. "Come on Bill. Ma will love this," he muttered.

The man led the horse to where she was lying and she sat up more terrified still.

"I can't possibly go with you, sir!" she whispered as loud as possible.

He smiled and chuckled. "Well, sweetheart... what do you plan on doin'? Feedin' the coyotes?" He hunkered down looking directly into her face. "Or... there are all kinds of worse things you could feed..." Then his smile turned into a frown as he looked at the ground around her. "Do you feel anything crawlin' on you anywhere, girl?"

She thought it an odd question but answered, "No."

He pulled her up until she was sitting straight and began running his hand over her back and through her hair. She realized that her shirtwaist was torn because she could feel his hands on the exposed skin of her shoulders. She gasped as she looked down and saw that it was also torn in front and gaped open exposing her entire collarbone.

As the frown on his face intensified the man quickly ran his hand over her back once more then moved to her waist. She instinctively moved to slap him, but he caught her hand and looked angrily into her face.

"I ain't out for a good time, sweetheart," he growled through clenched teeth. He pushed her back down and she wanted to weep when he lifted up her skirts and began feeling her right leg. But her state of severe dehydration prevented any tears from even developing.

"Well, you certainly ain't from around here," the man stated as he unfastened her bustle throwing it aside. "Women don't bother too much with these contraptions 'round these parts." Then he stopped. "Don't move," he commanded and she obeyed as she felt something crawling on her flesh under the left leg of her pantaloons.

She watched with utter mortification as the stranger's hand slowly slid beneath the cloth of her pantaloons and toward her knee. His hand clamped around something and he quickly withdrew it.

"Sorry little cuss!" he mumbled as he threw something to the ground and drew a large knife from his boot.

She then witnessed him smashing a large, sandy colored scorpion into the dirt with his well-worn boot. When she looked up again it was in time to see him cut the palm of his hand with the knife and begin sucking on the wound. He did this several times, spitting his own blood from his mouth each time.

"That sorry little cuss stung me," he mumbled. "They don't usually kill you, unless you're allergic or somethin'. But they make you awful sick and the sting gets terrible sore." He looked at her oddly for a moment. "You feel like you're gonna faint or somethin'?" he asked.

She swallowed hard and shook her head to dispel the awful dizziness in it. The man slipped the knife back into his boot and pulled her up to a sitting position again.

"Well, least you had sense enough to nearly drop dead 'round here," he muttered.

She watched as he pulled an odd shaped plant from the ground and broke open a few of the strange looking leaves. He squeezed out a slimy substance and began to apply it to her face. It smelled unpleasant, but felt very cool and soothing.

When he finished, he wiped his hand on his dusty trousers and said, "Now, let's see if you can sit a horse."

He pulled her to her feet, but her knees buckled and her mind began swimming. He caught her and sat her down again.

"I'm sorry," she whispered, wishing she could cry.

"Hang on there a minute," he said, with a hint more of kindness in his voice.

She watched, perfectly alarmed, as he actually proceeded to remove his shirt and wet it with water from the canteen. Even more disgraceful was the fact that he wore no form of undergarment beneath! None whatsoever! He was standing there bare from the waist up! And judging from the bronze color of his torso, he paraded around in such a state often.

When he looked at her again she covered her eyes with her sore hands.

He chuckled. "I believe you're blushin' under that sunburn, girl. You're definitely from somewhere else."

He draped the wet shirt over her head and shoulders and pulled her to her feet yet again. She still needed a great deal of support to stand. She tried to push herself away when her hands touched his bare chest as they searched for support.

"Tarnation, girl," he grumbled, taking her hands in his. "This is no time for propriety." She thought the word sounded a little out of character with his odd, rather Southern sounding accent.

He proceeded to run her hands from his shoulders slowly down and over his solid stomach. "See don't feel any different than your baby brother. You must be an unmarried one as well." He steadied her again. "Now, let's get you home to Mama so she can see the damage." He then lifted her onto the horse which sneezed and stomped his foreleg several times.

"Settle down, Bill. She's with me." He mounted behind her and pulled her tightly against his body. "Try not to fall off...it ain't far."

She was still too shocked by her recent lesson in anatomy to take much notice of the shameful way she sat astride the horse. But, somehow she knew, that until that moment, she had always ridden sidesaddle. A great wave of fatigue was overtaking her and she couldn't help but let her head fall back against his shoulder.

"I'm sorry," she whispered. "I think I'm going to faint." She felt his arm tighten around her waist and the heat of his breath on her face as he spoke in her ear.

"It ain't far, girl. Now listen here, I'm Jackson McCall. This here feller you're on is Bill. He don't care much for nobody but me...so you sit real still and hang on tight."

She could smell leather, bacon, and perspiration... but it was somehow a pleasant and comforting combination. "Yes, sir," she whispered, trying to keep her eyes open.

"Yes, sir?" he repeated in an astonished whisper. "Where are you from, girl?"

She tried and tried to pull an answer from her fevered brain. But she truly couldn't.

"I don't know," she whispered, just before she gave into the need to be unconscious.

My everlasting admiration, gratitude, and love…
To my husband, Kevin…
Proof that heroes really *do* exist!
I Love You!

ABOUT THE AUTHOR

Marcia Lynn McClure's intoxicating succession of novels, novellas, and e-books—including *The Visions of Ransom Lake*, *A Crimson Frost*, *The Pirate Ruse*, and most recently *The Chimney Sweep Charm*—has established her as one of the most favored and engaging authors of true romance. Her unprecedented forte in weaving captivating stories of western, medieval, regency, and contemporary amour void of brusque intimacy has earned her the title "The Queen of Kissing."

Marcia, who was born in Albuquerque, New Mexico, has spent her life intrigued with people, history, love, and romance. A wife, mother, grandmother, family historian, poet, and author, Marcia Lynn McClure spins her tales of splendor for the sake of offering respite through the beauty, mirth, and delight of a worthwhile and wonderful story.

BIBLIOGRAPHY

Beneath the Honeysuckle Vine
A Better Reason to Fall in Love
Born for Thorton's Sake
The Chimney Sweep Charm
A Crimson Frost
Daydreams
Desert Fire
Divine Deception
Dusty Britches
The Fragrance of her Name
The Haunting of Autumn Lake
The Heavenly Surrender
The Highwayman of Tanglewood
Kiss in the Dark
Kissing Cousins
The Light of the Lovers' Moon
Love Me
The McCall Trilogy
An Old-Fashioned Romance
The Pirate Ruse
The Prairie Prince
The Rogue Knight
Romantic Vignettes-The Anthology of Premiere
Novellas
Saphyre Snow
Shackles of Honor
Sudden Storms
Sweet Cherry Ray

Take a Walk With Me
The Tide of the Mermaid Tears
The Time of Aspen Falls
To Echo the Past
The Touch of Sage
The Trove of the Passion Room
Untethered
The Visions of Ransom Lake
Weathered Too Young
The Whispered Kiss
The Windswept Flame